Mighty Mighty MONSTERS

My
MISSING
MONSTER

STONE ARCH BOOKS
a capstone imprint

My MISSING MONSTER

created by Sean O'Reilly
illustrated by Arcana Studio

Mighty Mighty Monsters are published by Stone Arch Books, A Capstone Imprint
151 Good Counsel Drive, P.O. Box 669 Mankato, Minnesota 56002 *www.capstonepub.com*

Library of Congress Cataloging-in-Publication Data
O'Reilly, Sean, 1974-
  My missing monster / written by Sean O'Reilly ; illustrated by Arcana Studio.
    p. cm. -- (Mighty Mighty Monsters)
  Summary: When one of their pets goes missing, the Mighty Mighty Monsters all join in
the search.
  ISBN 978-1-4342-2153-7 (library binding)
  1. Graphic novels. [1. Graphic novels. 2. Monsters--Fiction. 3. Pets--Fiction.] I. Arcana
Studio. II. Title.
  PZ7.7.O74My 2010
  741.5'973--dc22   2010004130

Printed in the United States of America in Stevens Point, Wisconsin.
032010
005741WZF10

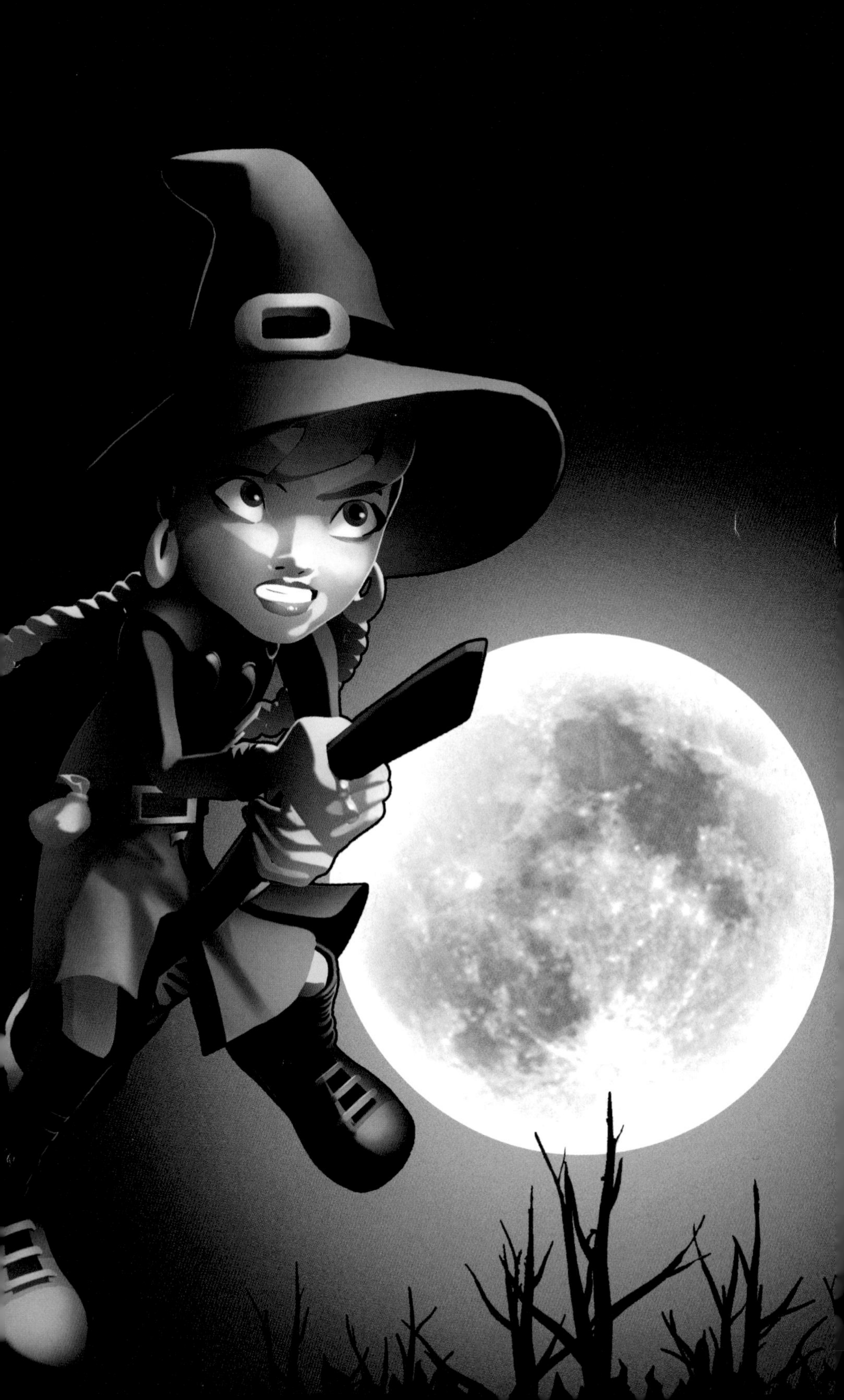

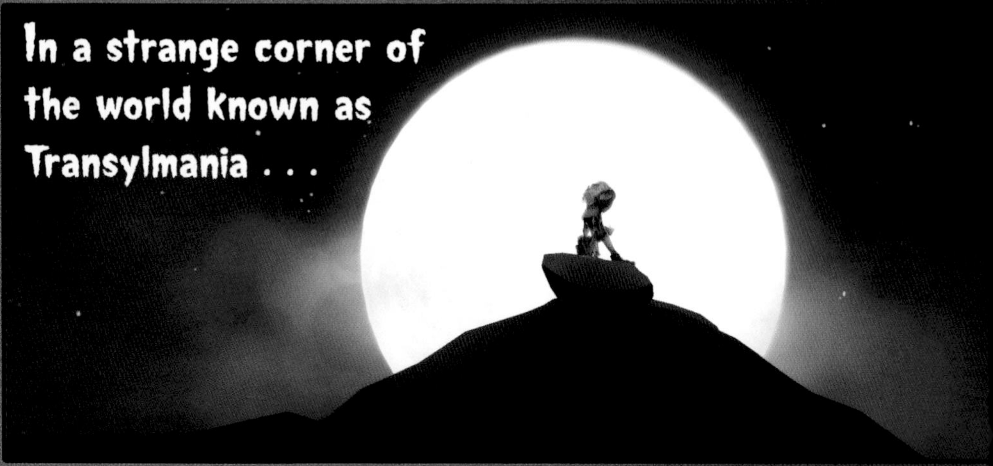
In a strange corner of the world known as Transylmania . . .

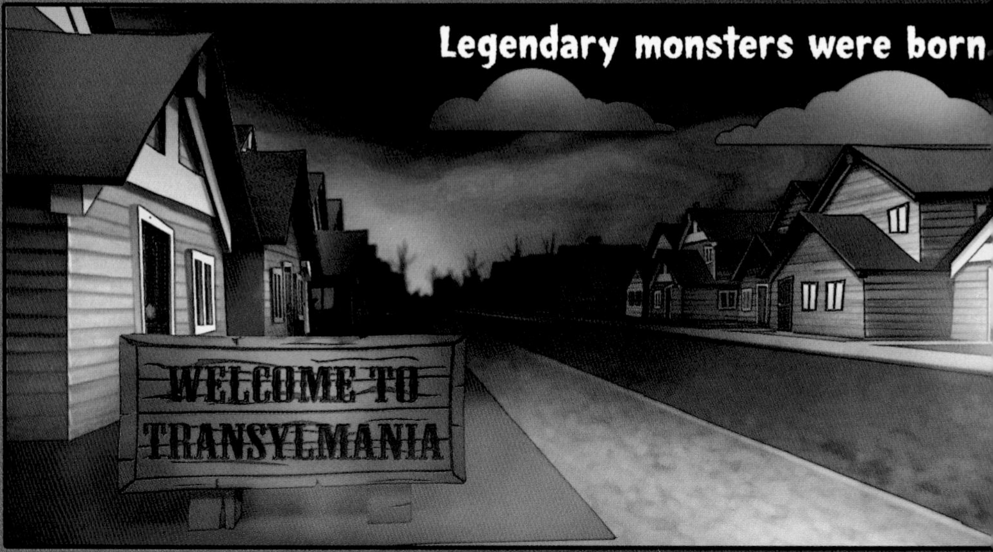
Legendary monsters were born
WELCOME TO
TRANSYLMANIA

But long before their frightful fame, these classic creatures faced fears of their own.

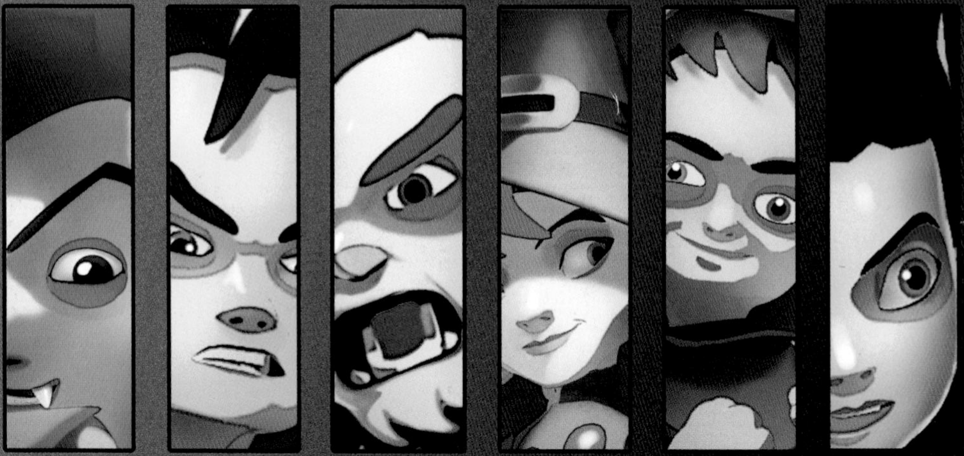

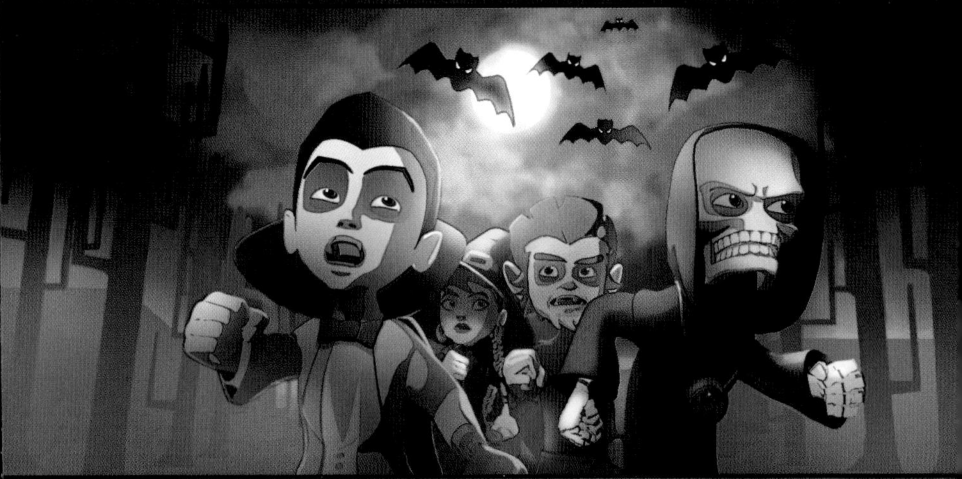

To take on terrifying teachers and homework horrors, they formed the most fearsome friendship on Earth .

Mighty Mighty MONSTERS

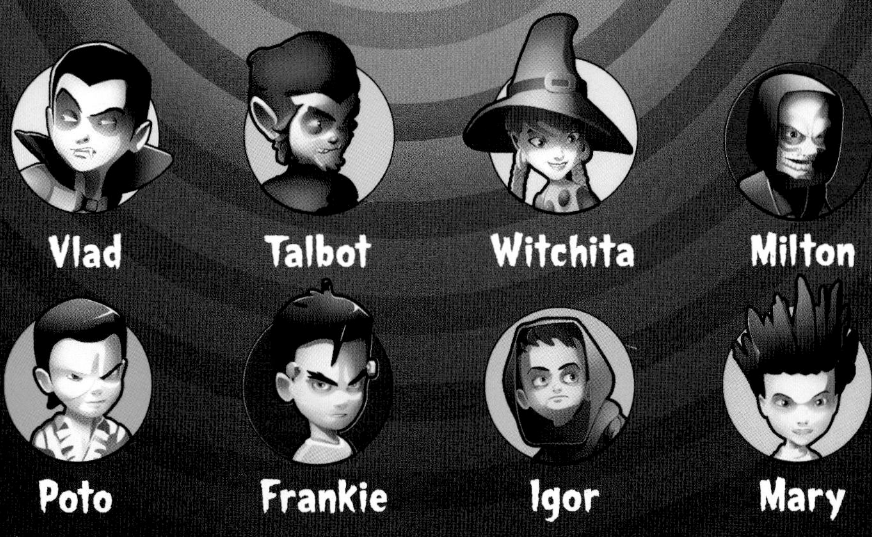

Vlad
Talbot
Witchita
Milton
Poto
Frankie
Igor
Mary

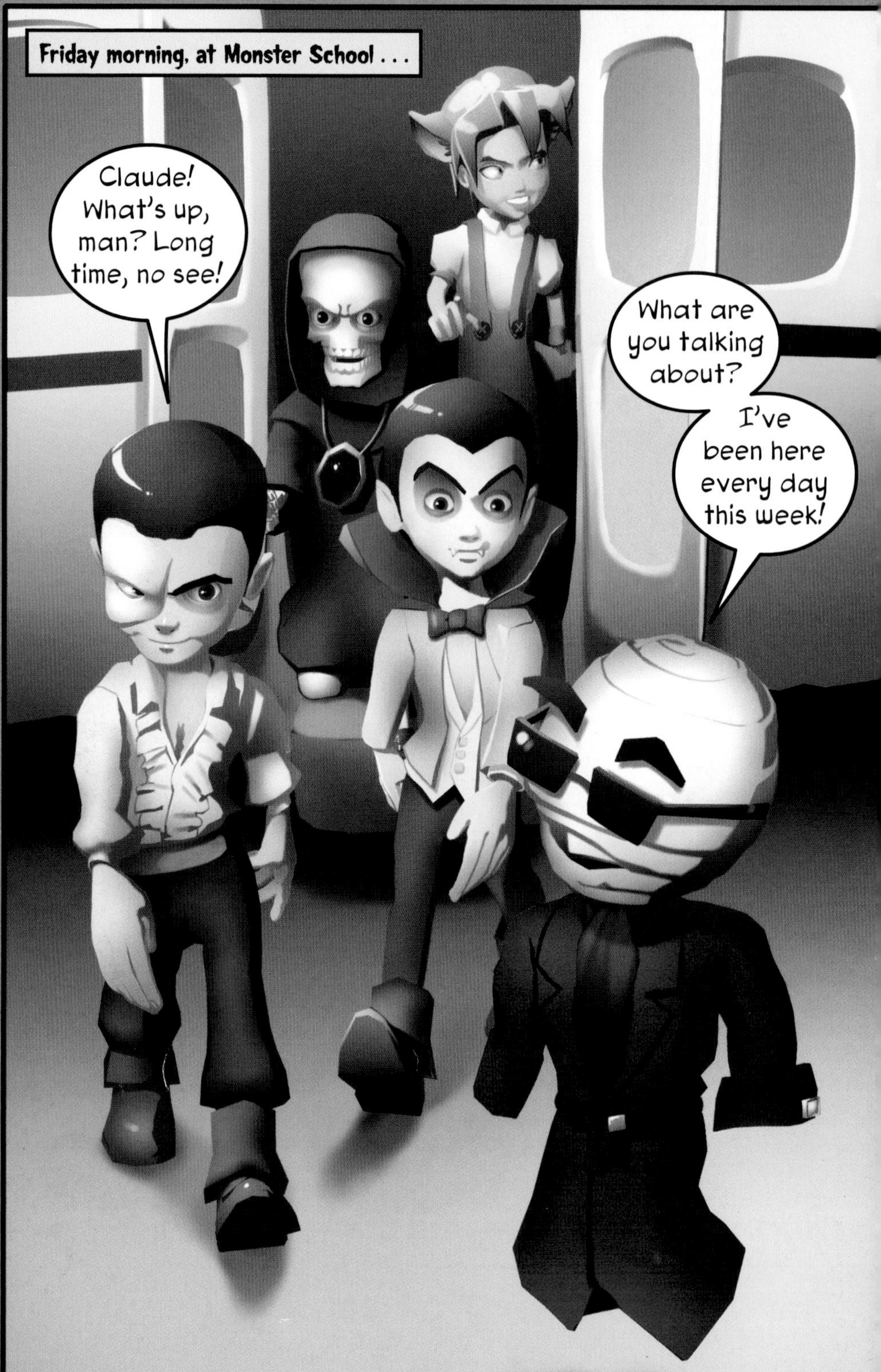
Friday morning, at Monster School . . .
Claude! What's up, man? Long time, no see!
What are you talking about?
I've been here every day this week!

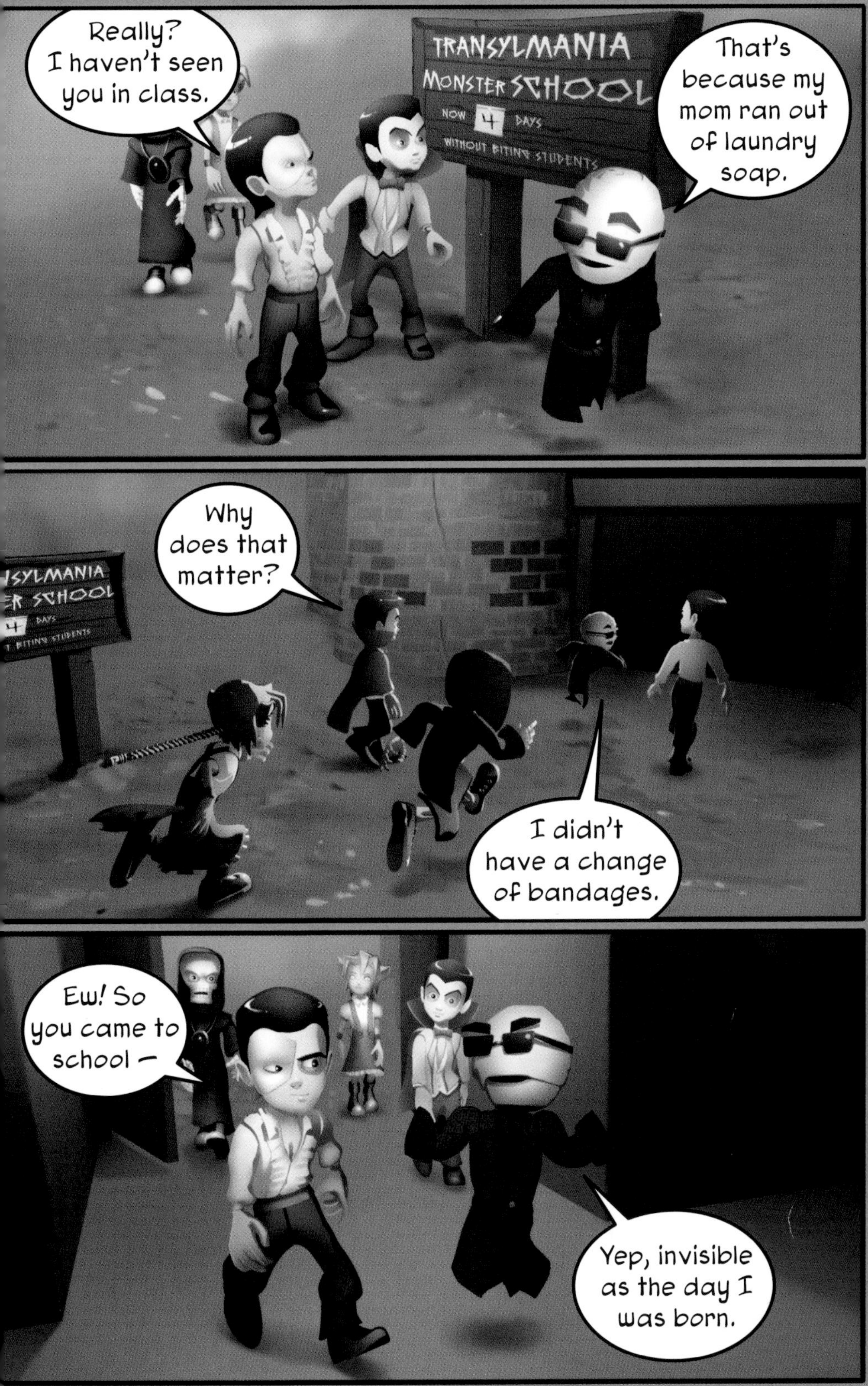
TRANSYLMANIA
MONSTER SCHOOL
NOW 4 DAYS
WITHOUT BITING STUDENTS
Really? I haven't seen you in class.
That's because my mom ran out of laundry soap.
Why does that matter?
I didn't have a change of bandages.
Ew! So you came to school –
Yep, invisible as the day I was born.

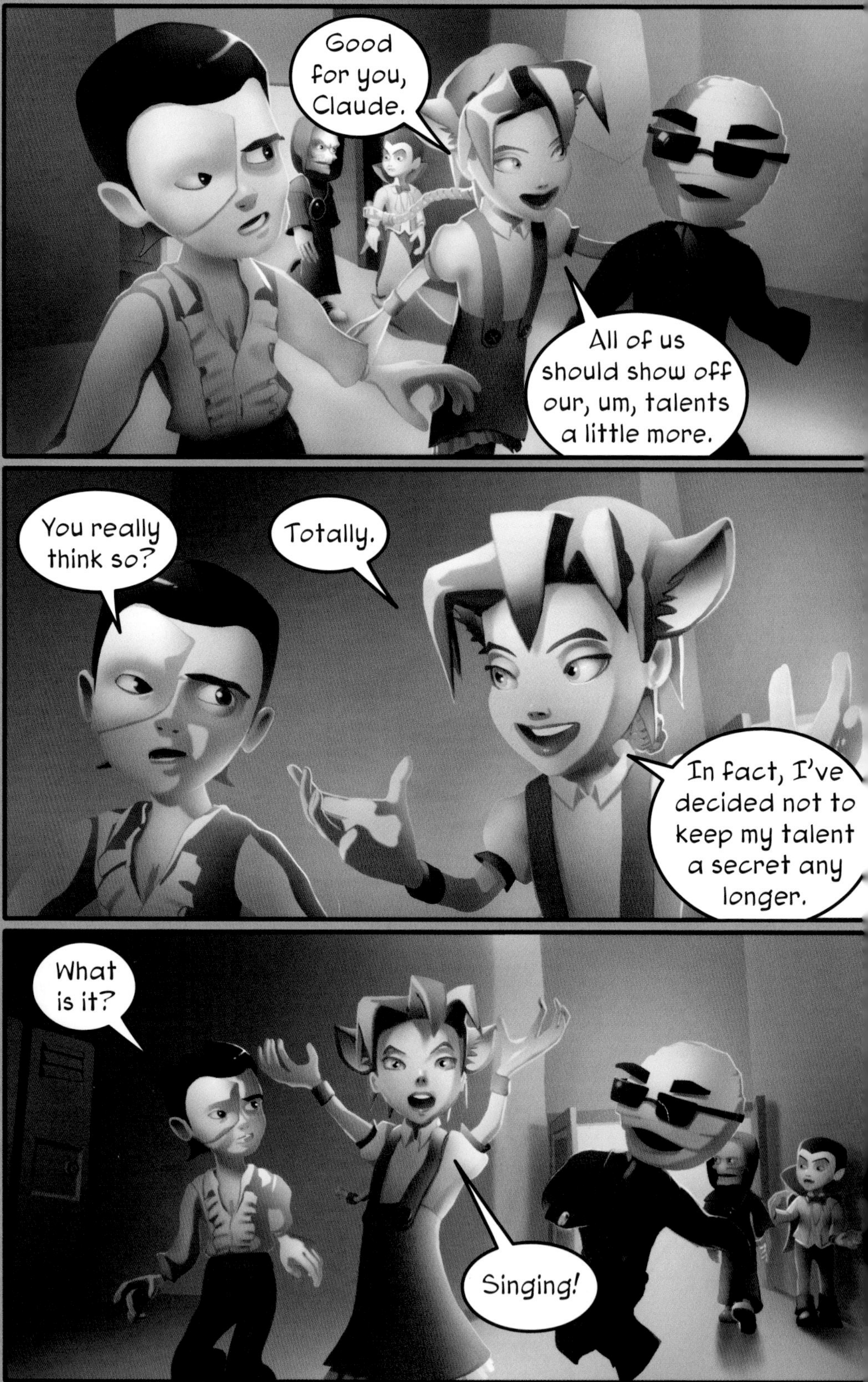
Good for you, Claude.
All of us should show off our, um, talents a little more.
You really think so?
Totally.
In fact, I've decided not to keep my talent a secret any longer.
What is it?
Singing!

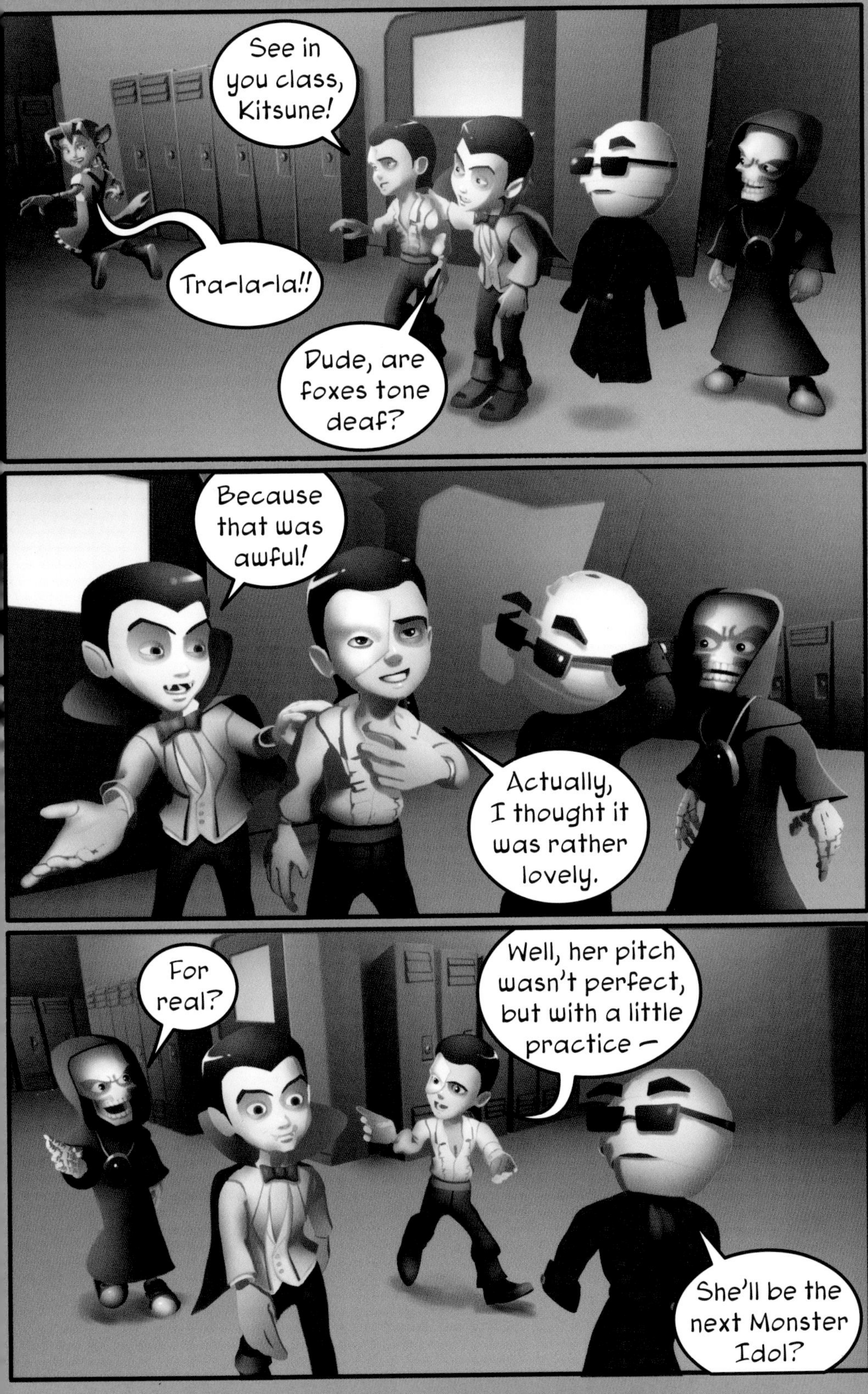

See in you class, Kitsune!
Tra-la-la!!
Dude, are foxes tone deaf?
Because that was awful!
Actually, I thought it was rather lovely.
For real?
Well, her pitch wasn't perfect, but with a little practice —
She'll be the next Monster Idol?

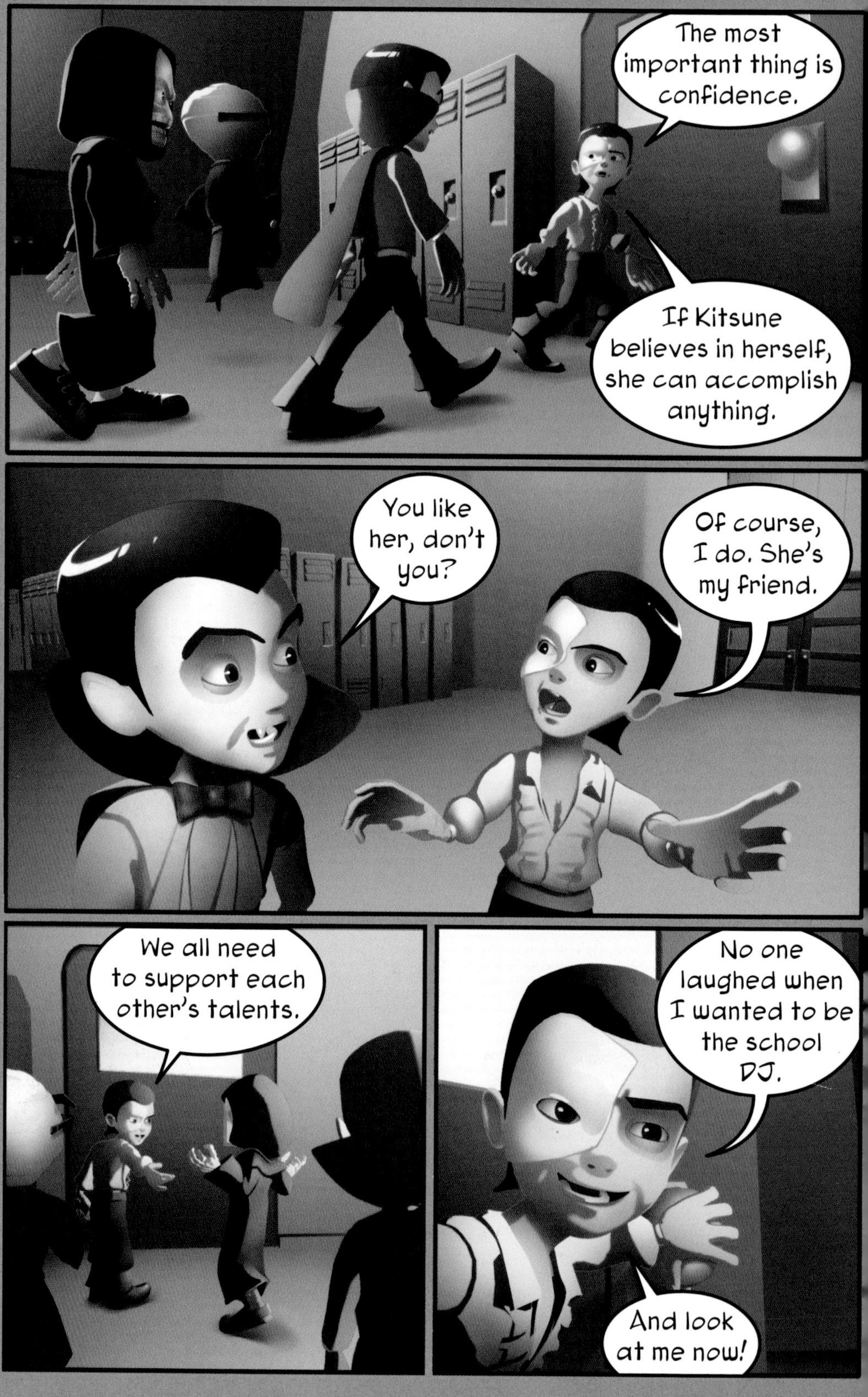
The most important thing is confidence.
If Kitsune believes in herself, she can accomplish anything.
You like her, don't you?
Of course, I do. She's my friend.
We all need to support each other's talents.
No one laughed when I wanted to be the school DJ.
And look at me now!

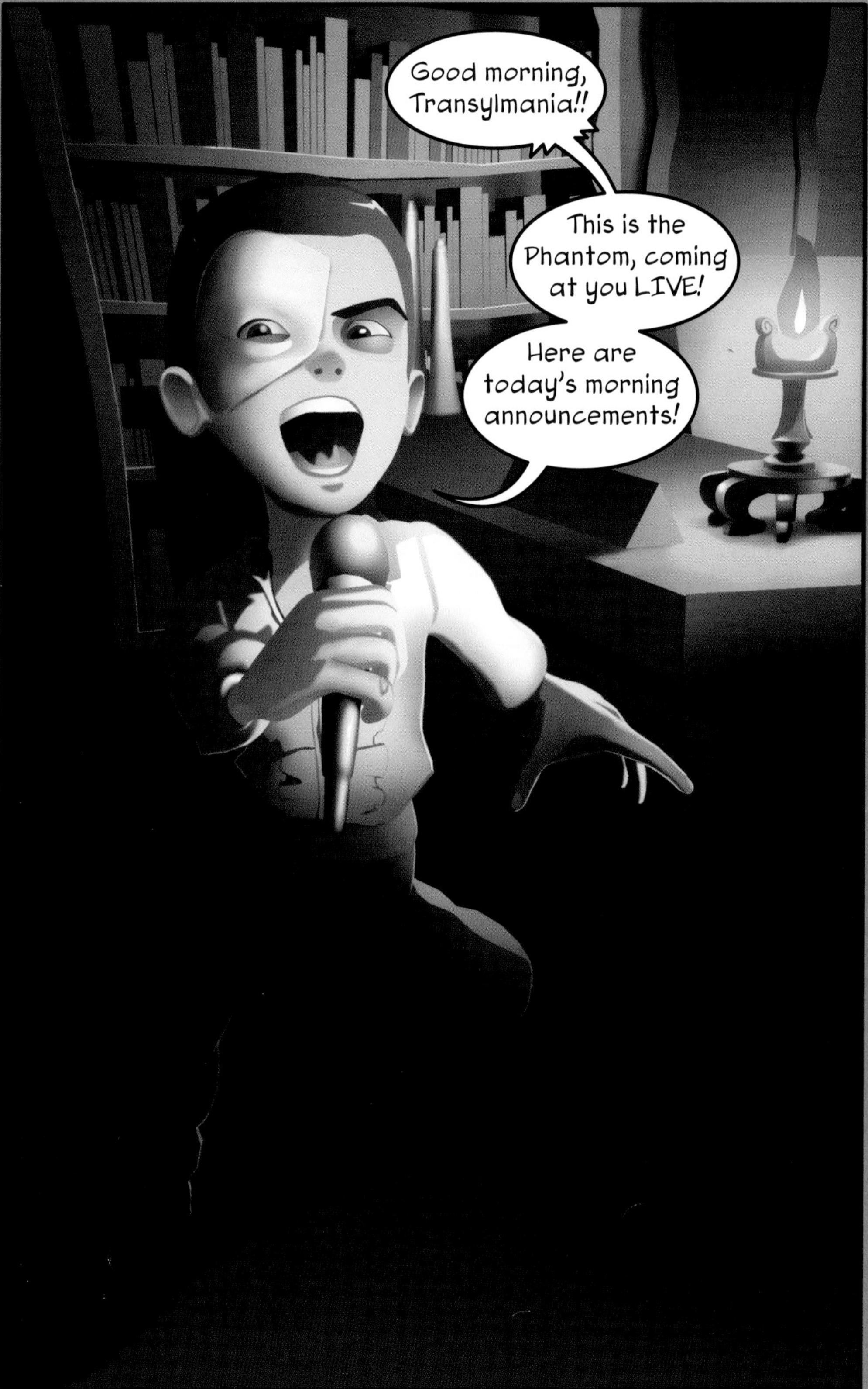
Good morning, Transylmania!!
This is the Phantom, coming at you LIVE!
Here are today's morning announcements!

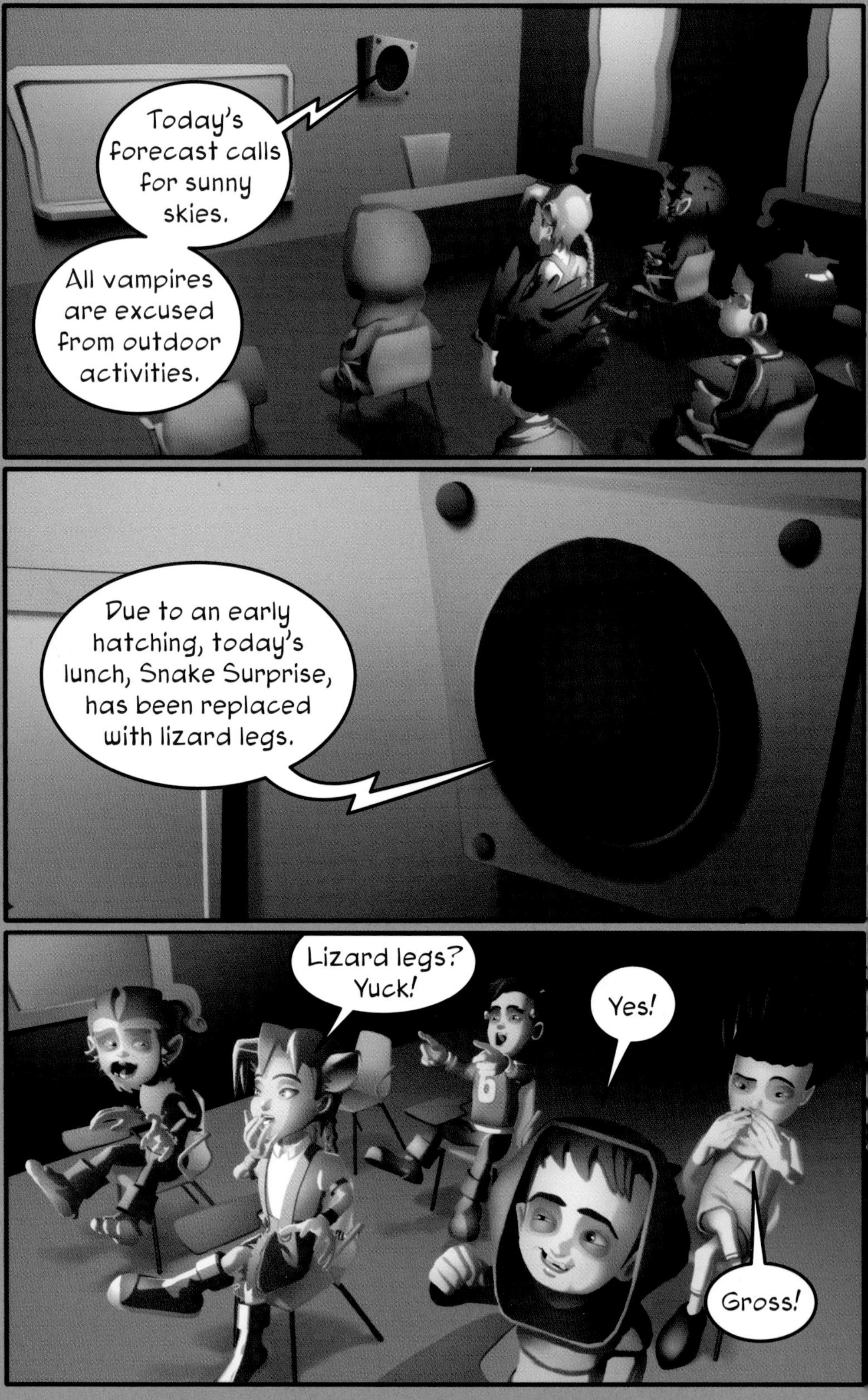
Today's forecast calls for sunny skies.
All vampires are excused from outdoor activities.
Due to an early hatching, today's lunch, Snake Surprise, has been replaced with lizard legs.
Lizard legs? Yuck!
Yes!
Gross!

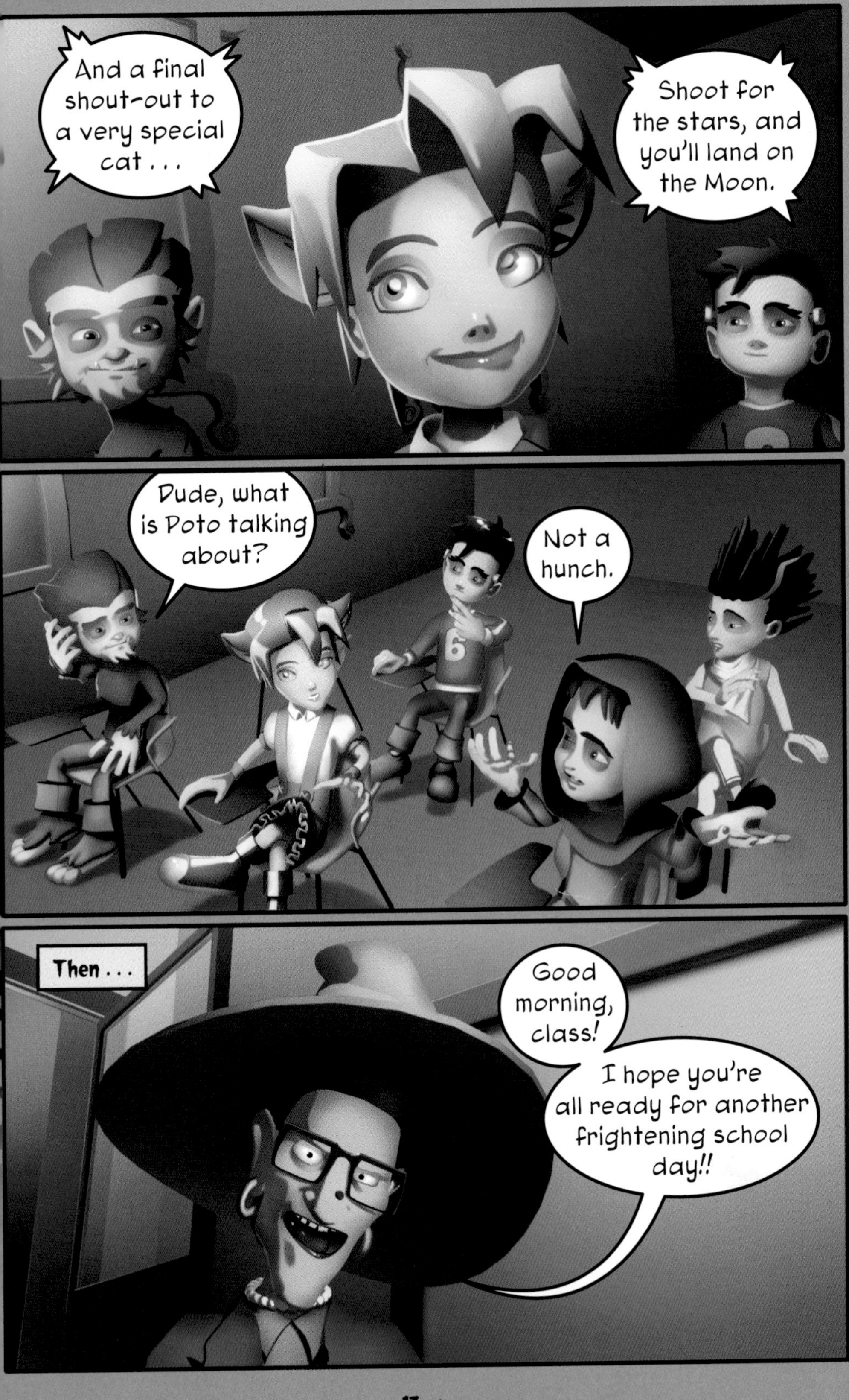
And a final shout-out to a very special cat . . .
Shoot for the stars, and you'll land on the Moon.
Dude, what is Poto talking about?
Not a hunch.
Then . . .
Good morning, class!
I hope you're all ready for another frightening school day!!

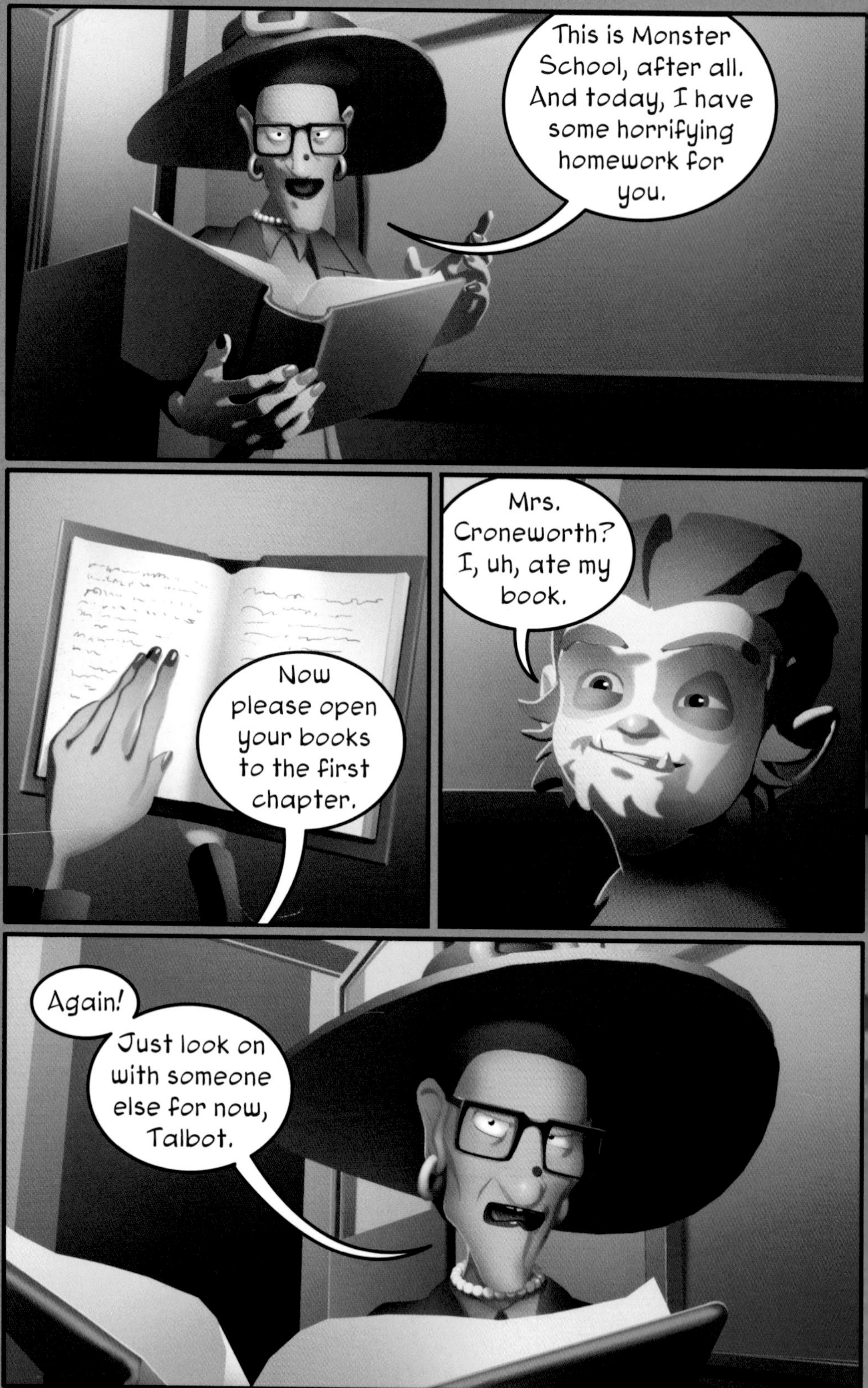
This is Monster School, after all. And today, I have some horrifying homework for you.
Now please open your books to the first chapter.
Mrs. Croneworth? I, uh, ate my book.
Again!
Just look on with someone else for now, Talbot.

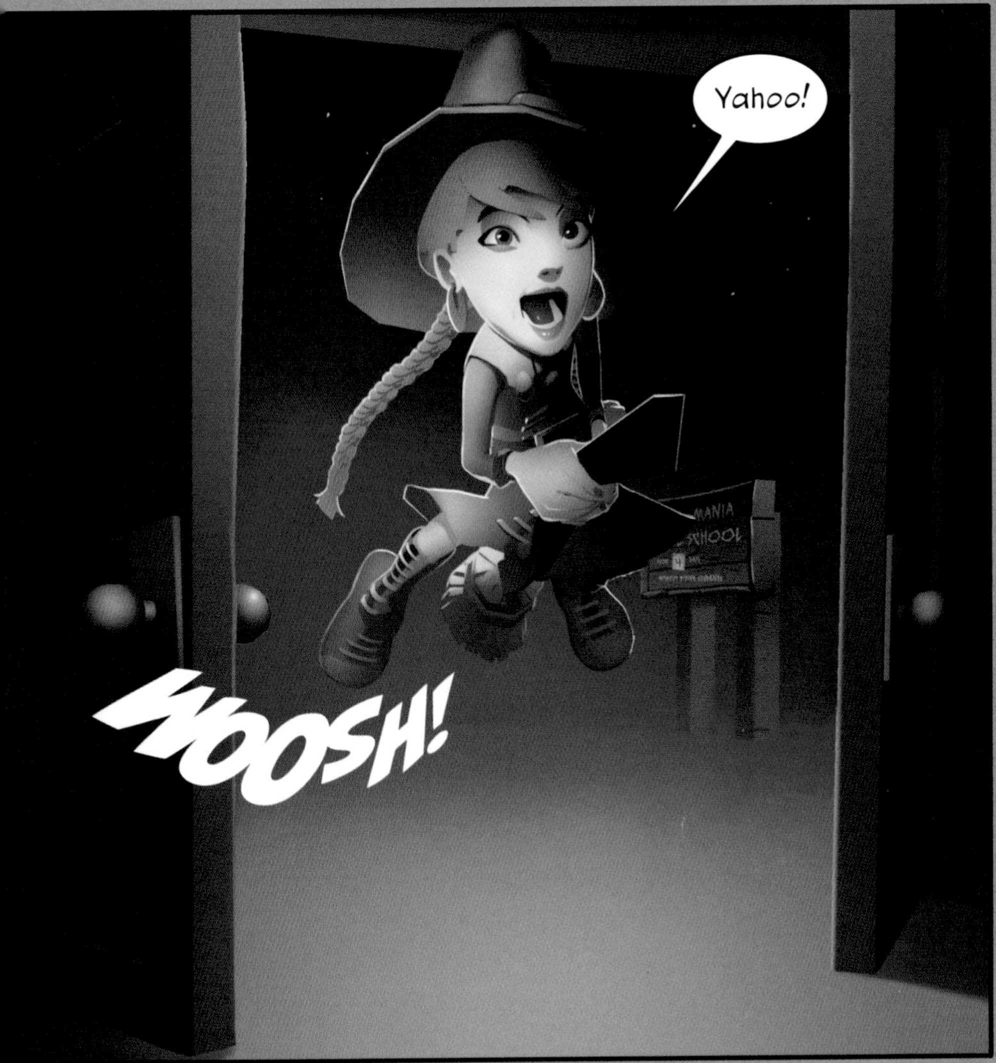
Yahoo!
WOOSH!

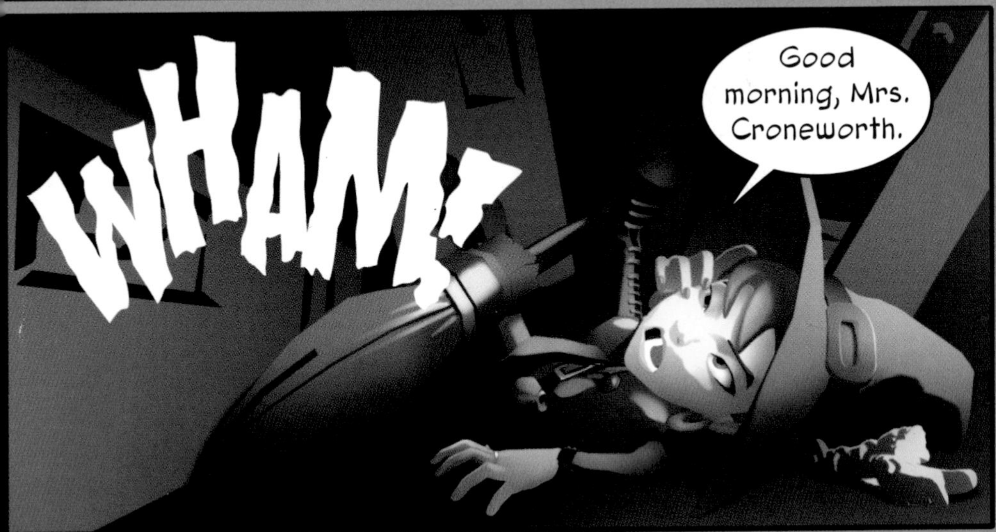
WHAM!
Good morning, Mrs. Croneworth.

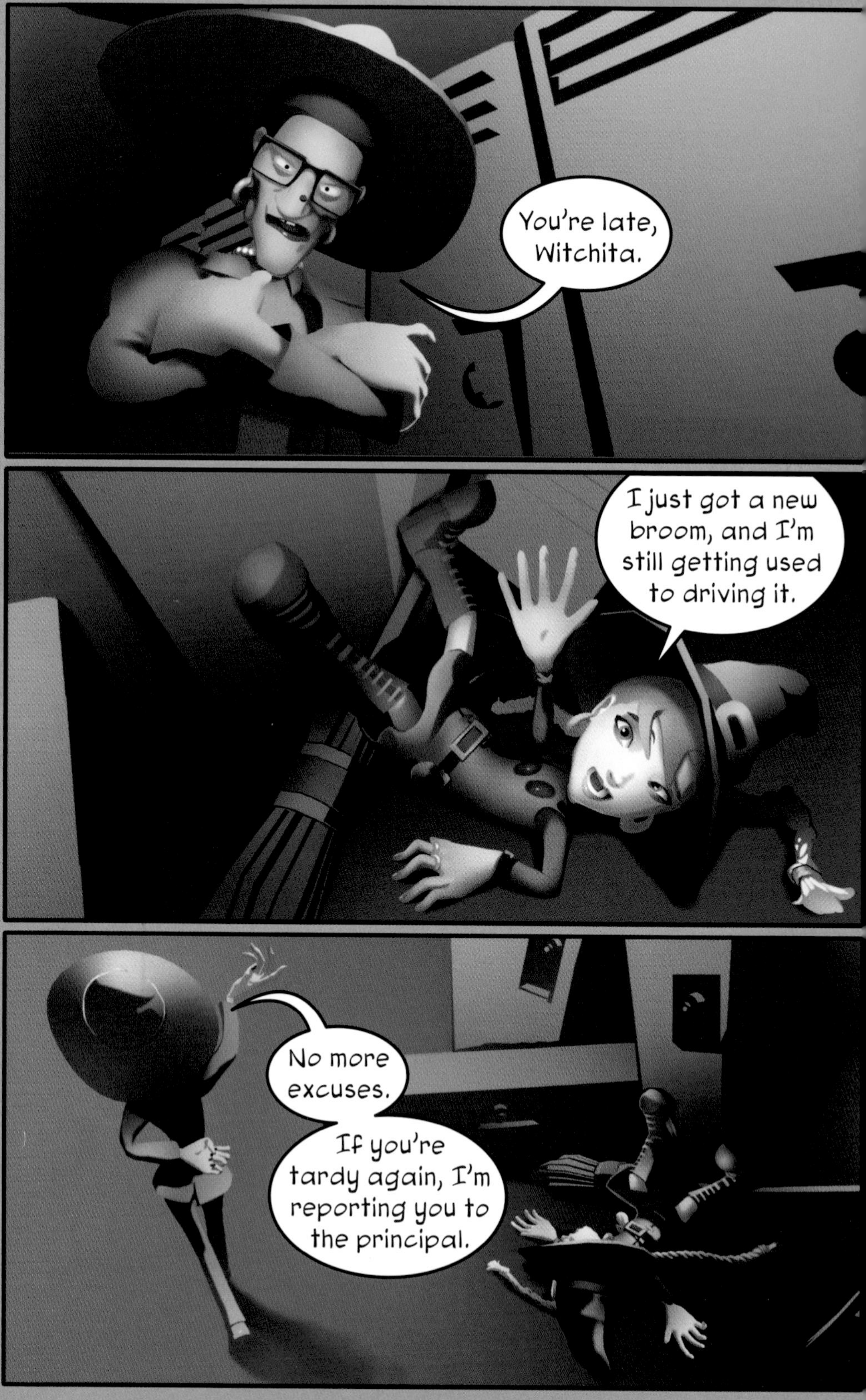
You're late, Witchita.
I just got a new broom, and I'm still getting used to driving it.
No more excuses.
If you're tardy again, I'm reporting you to the principal.

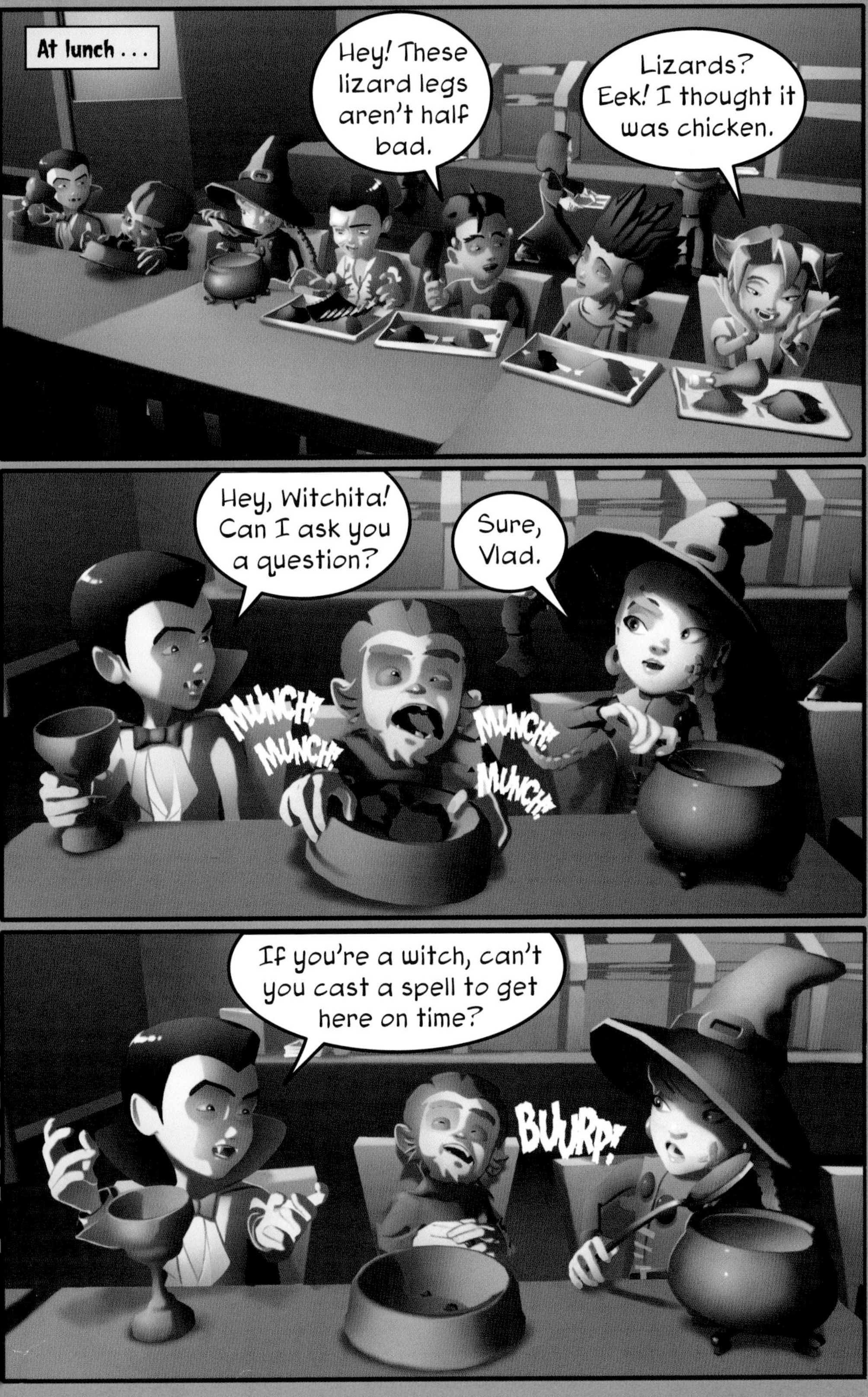
At lunch . . .
Hey! These lizard legs aren't half bad.
Lizards? Eek! I thought it was chicken.
Hey, Witchita! Can I ask you a question?
Sure, Vlad.
MUNCH! MUNCH!
MUNCH! MUNCH!
If you're a witch, can't you cast a spell to get here on time?
BUURP!

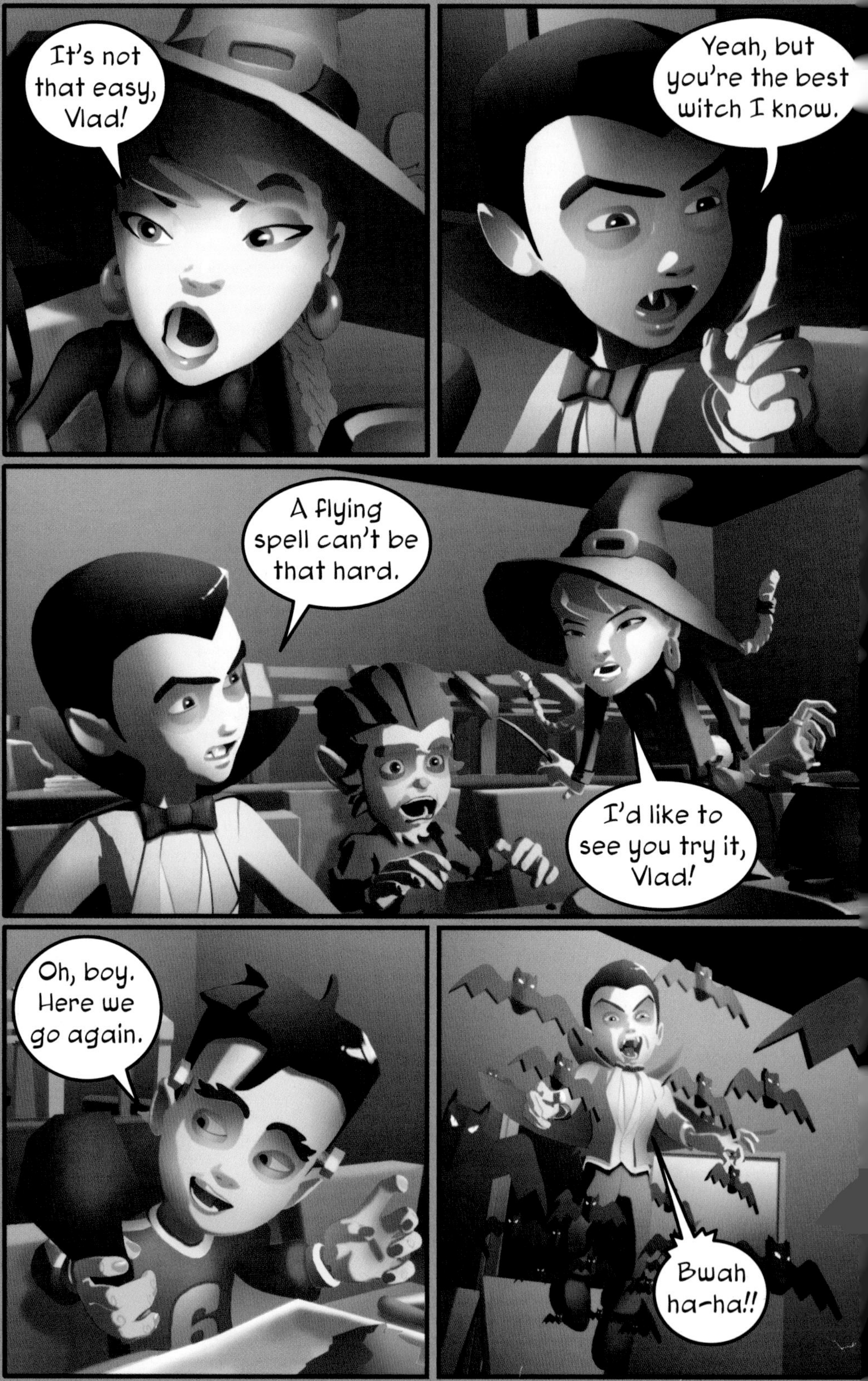
It's not that easy, Vlad!
Yeah, but you're the best witch I know.
A flying spell can't be that hard.
I'd like to see you try it, Vlad!
Oh, boy. Here we go again.
Bwah ha-ha!!

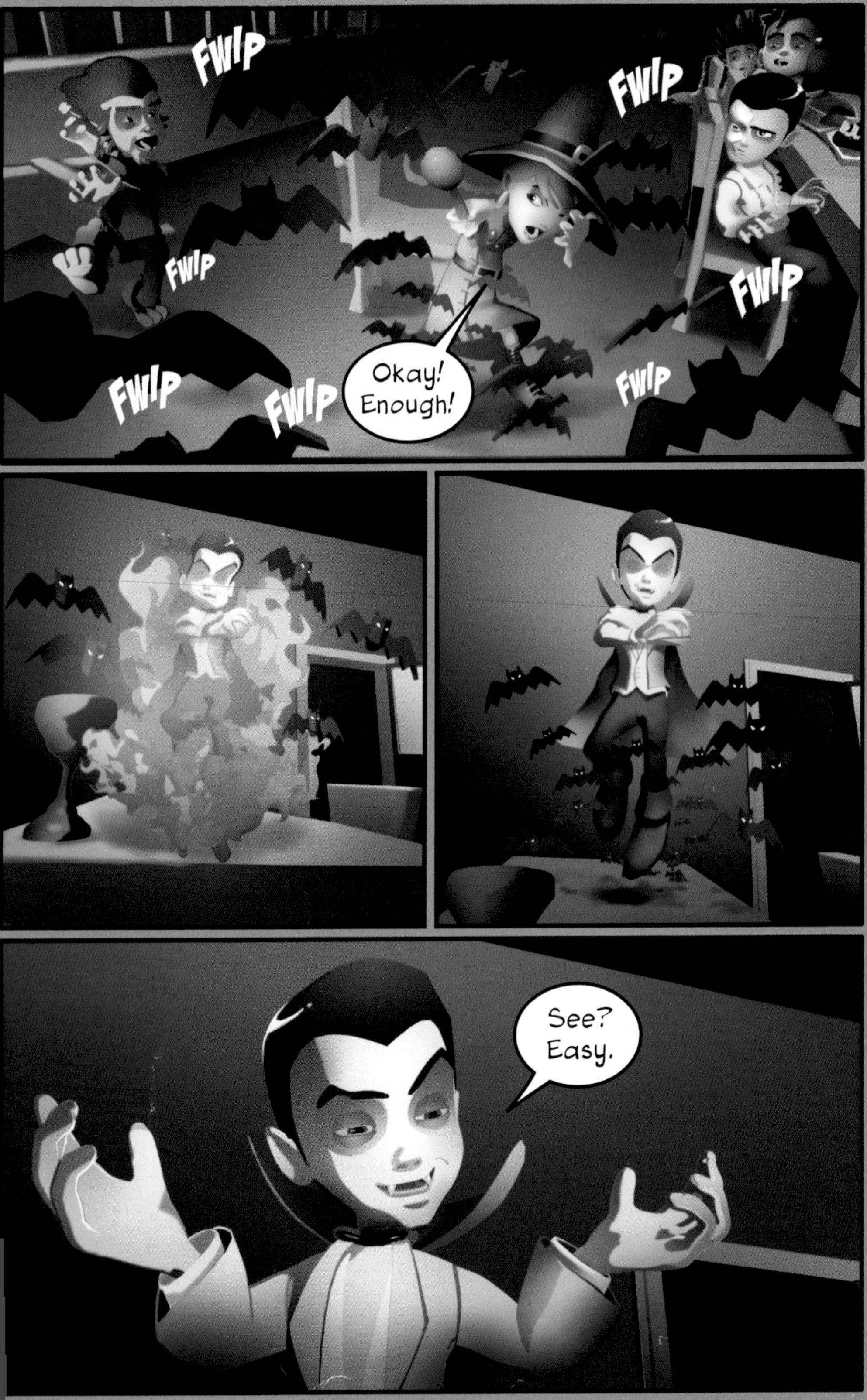
FWIP
FWIP
FWIP
FWIP
FWIP
FWIP
FWIP
Okay! Enough!
See? Easy.

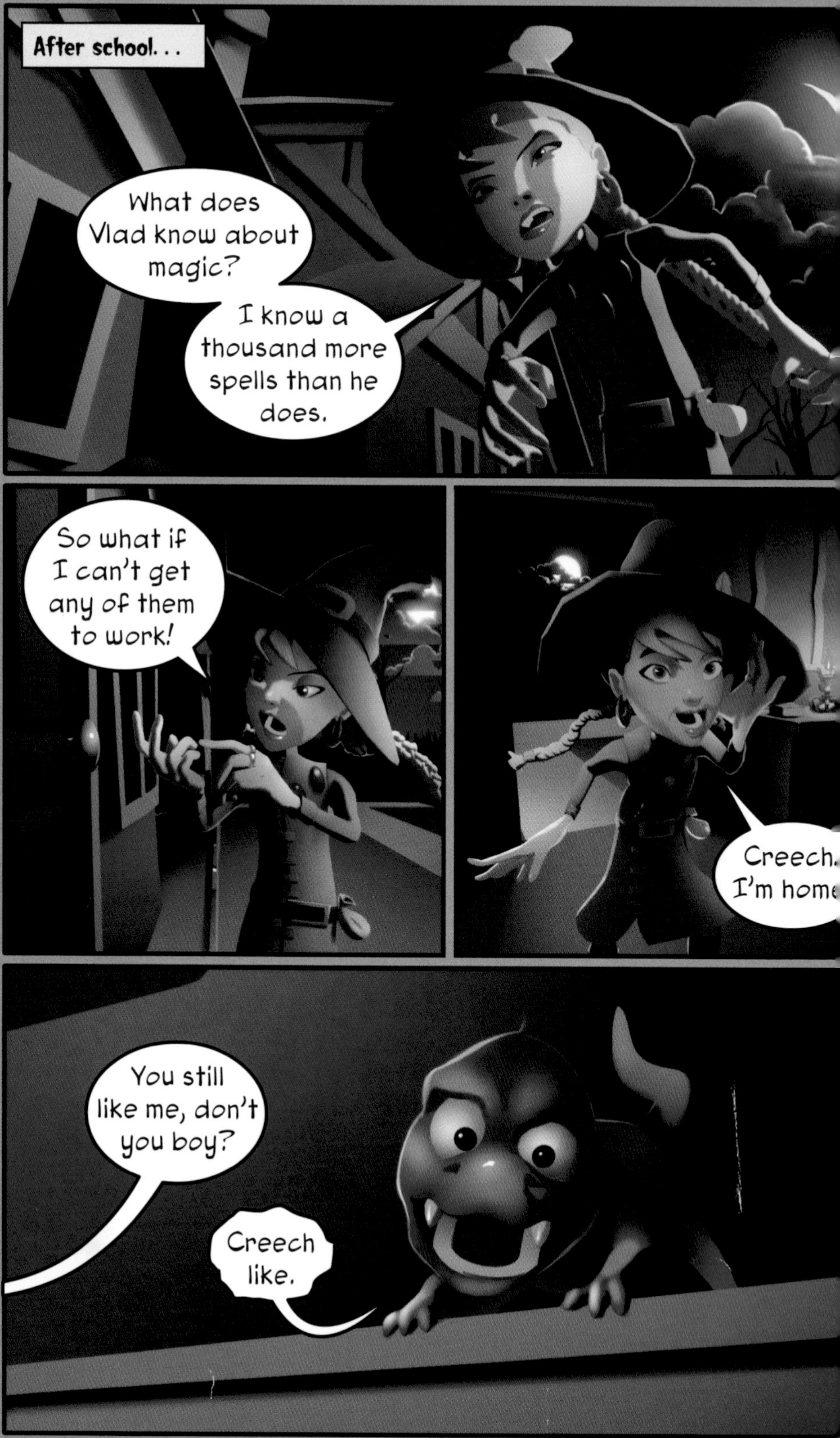
After school. . .
What does Vlad know about magic?
I know a thousand more spells than he does.
So what if I can't get any of them to work!
Creech. I'm home
You still like me, don't you boy?
Creech like.

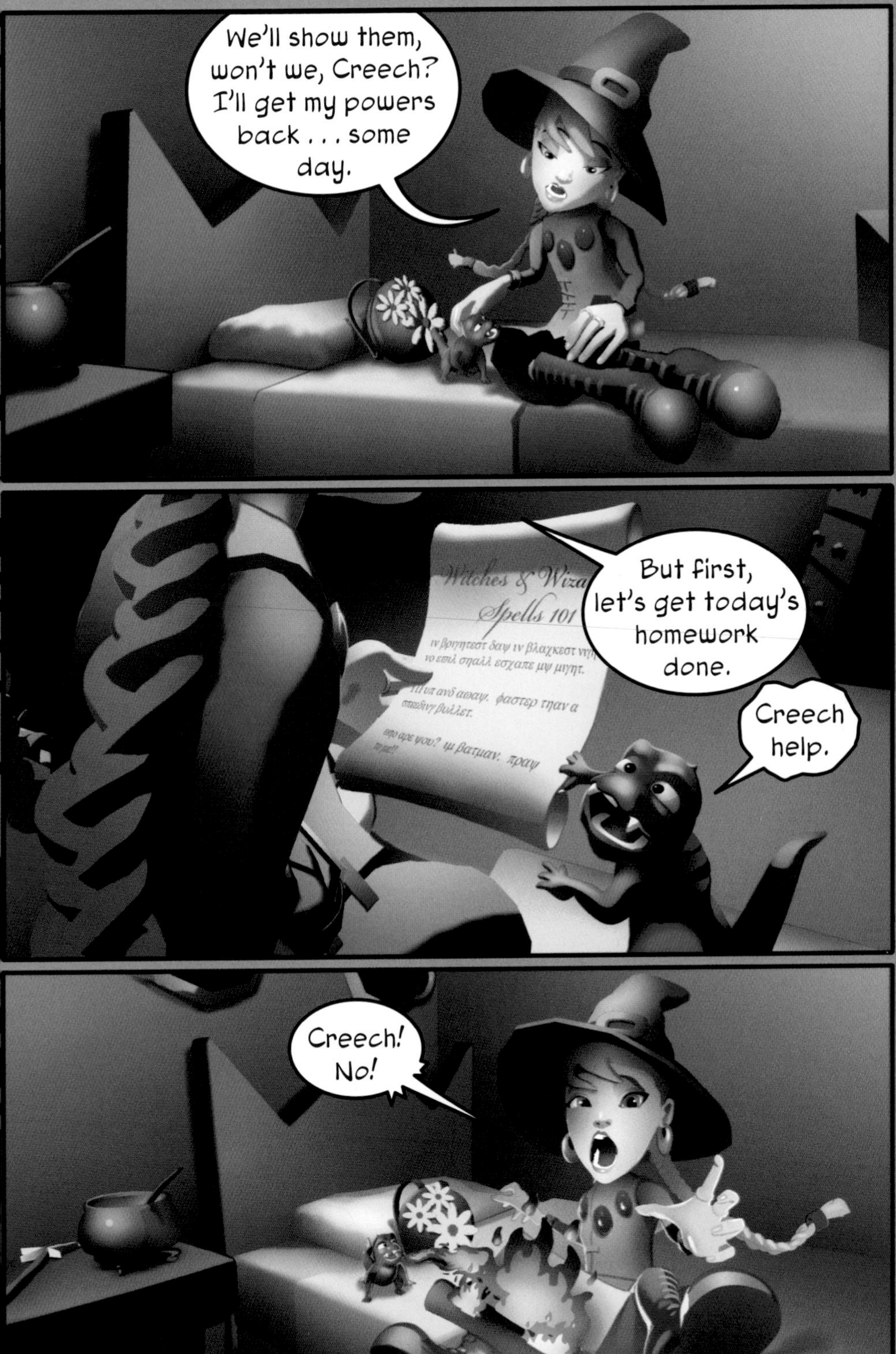
We'll show them, won't we, Creech? I'll get my powers back . . . some day.
Spells 101
But first, let's get today's homework done.
Creech help.
Creech! No!

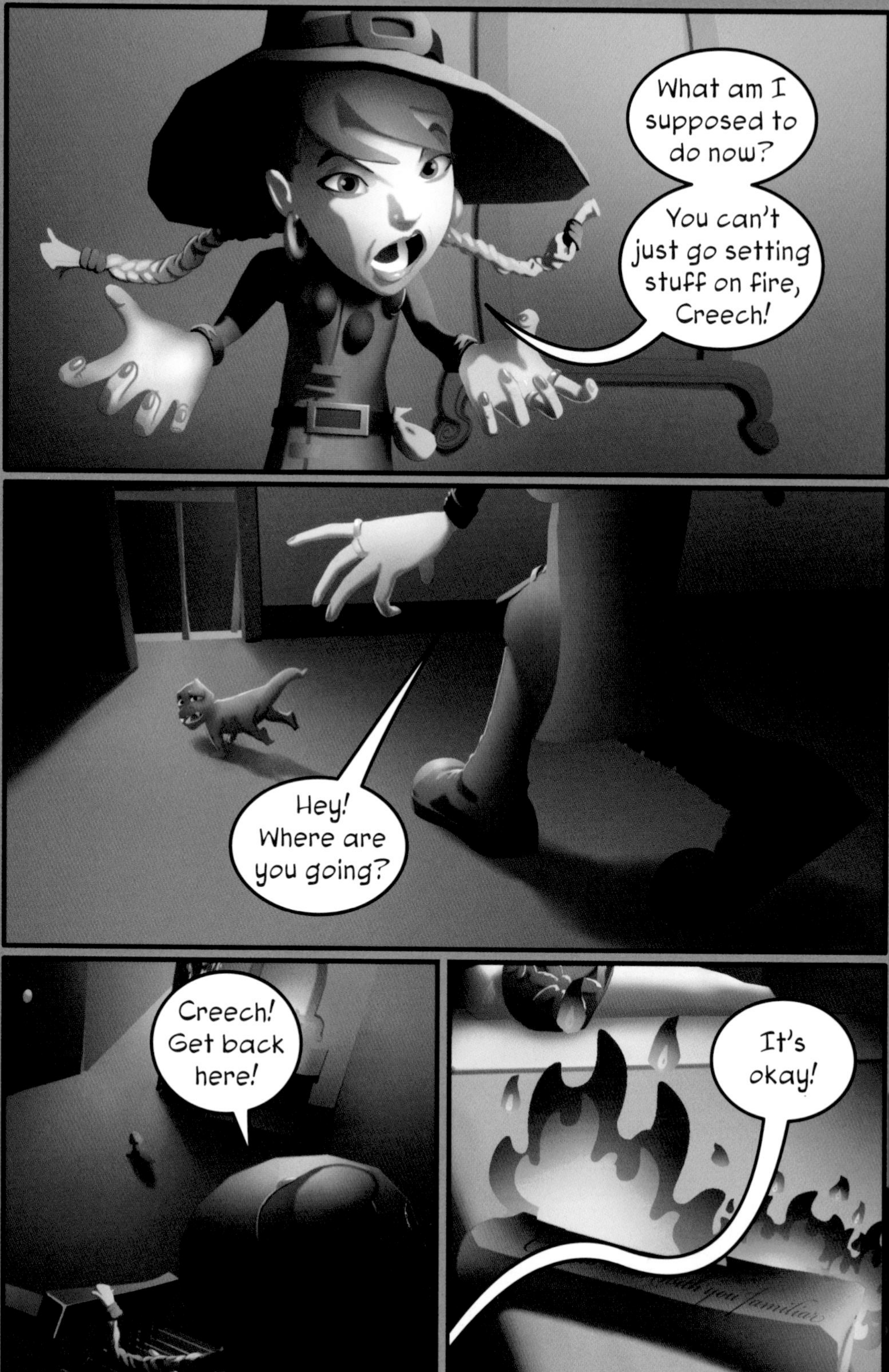
What am I supposed to do now?
You can't just go setting stuff on fire, Creech!
Hey! Where are you going?
Creech! Get back here!
It's okay!

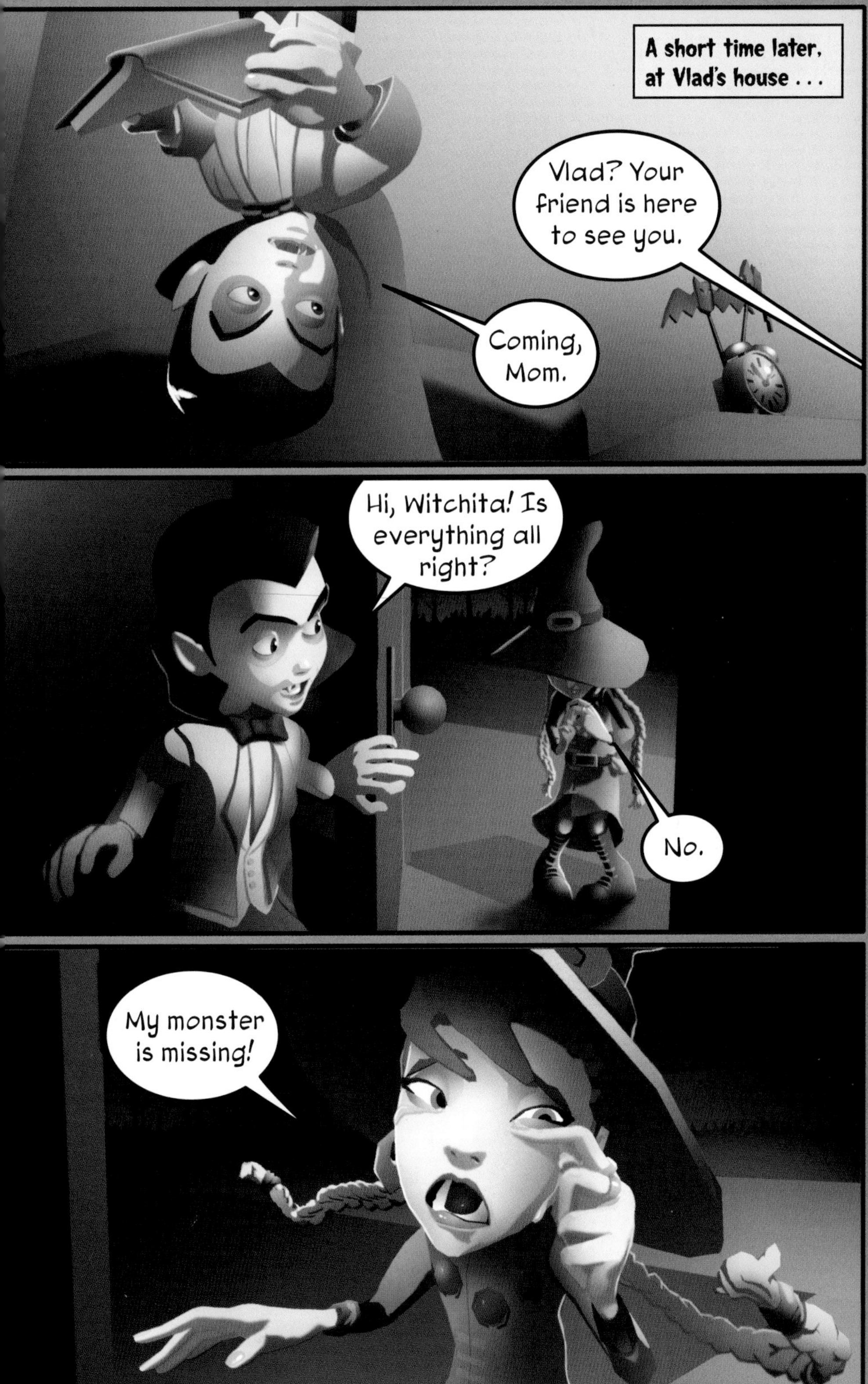
A short time later, at Vlad's house . . .
Vlad? Your friend is here to see you.
Coming, Mom.
Hi, Witchita! Is everything all right?
No.
My monster is missing!

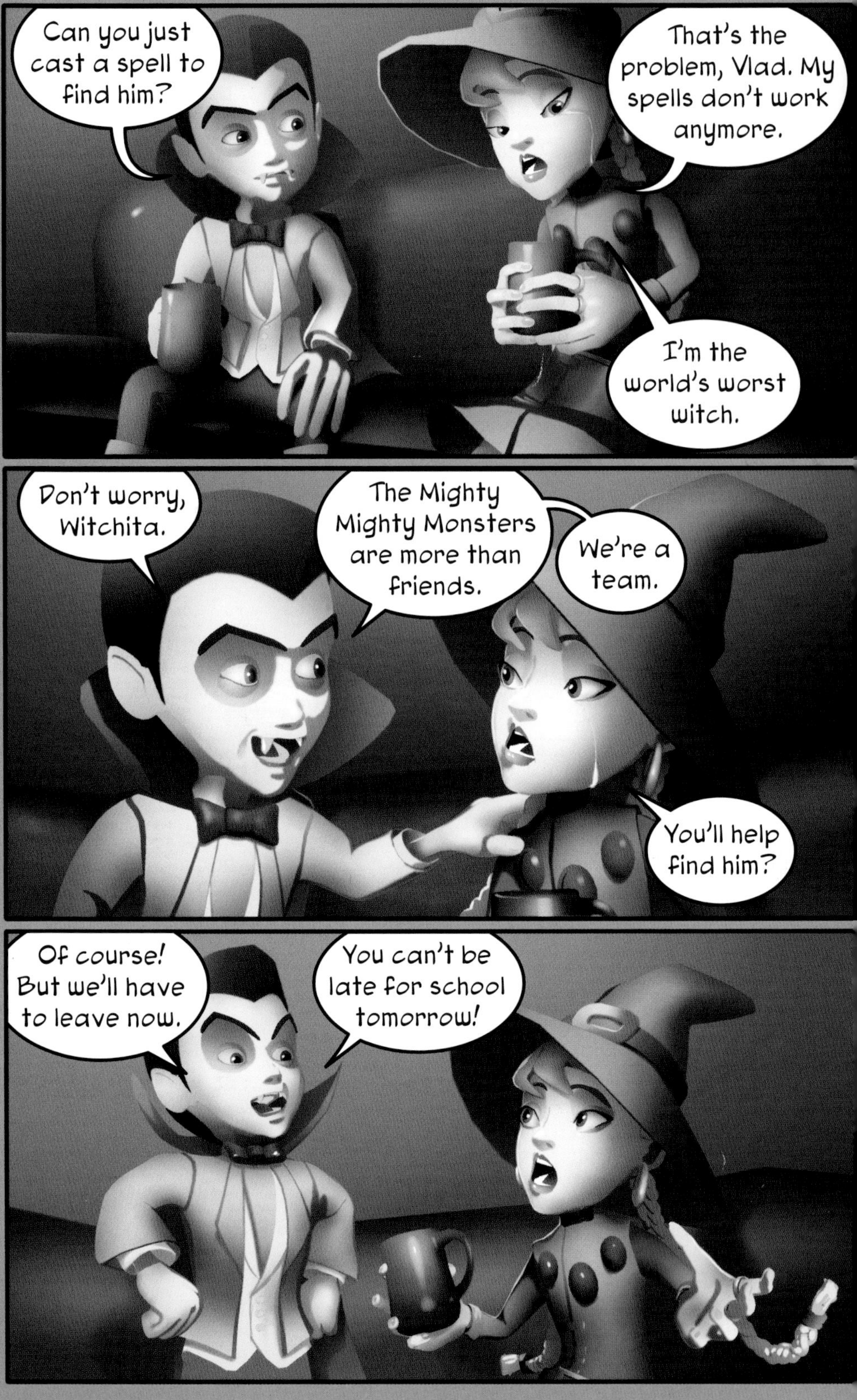
Can you just cast a spell to find him?
That's the problem, Vlad. My spells don't work anymore.
I'm the world's worst witch.
Don't worry, Witchita.
The Mighty Mighty Monsters are more than friends.
We're a team.
You'll help find him?
Of course! But we'll have to leave now.
You can't be late for school tomorrow!

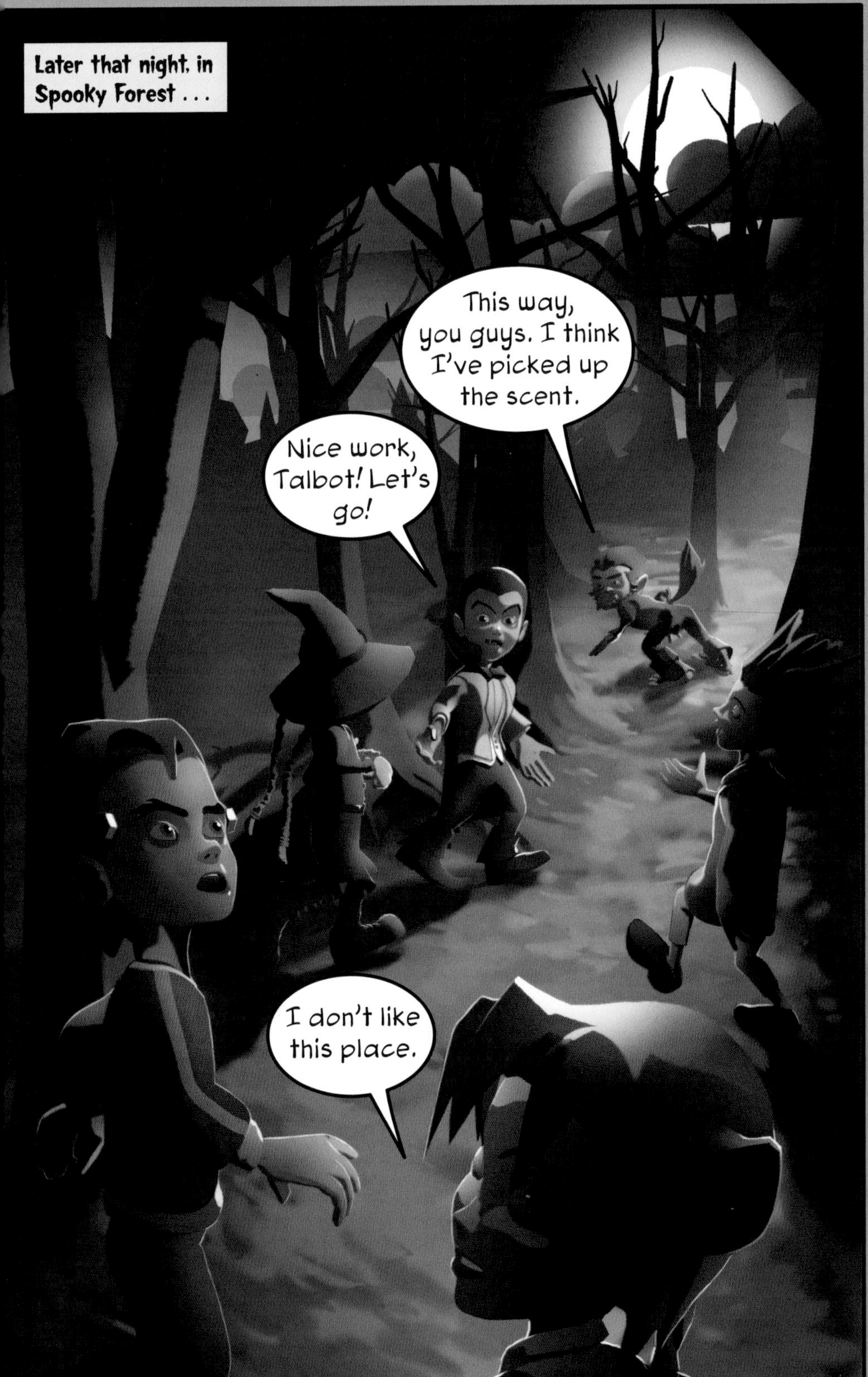
Later that night, in Spooky Forest . . .
This way, you guys. I think I've picked up the scent.
Nice work, Talbot! Let's go!
I don't like this place.

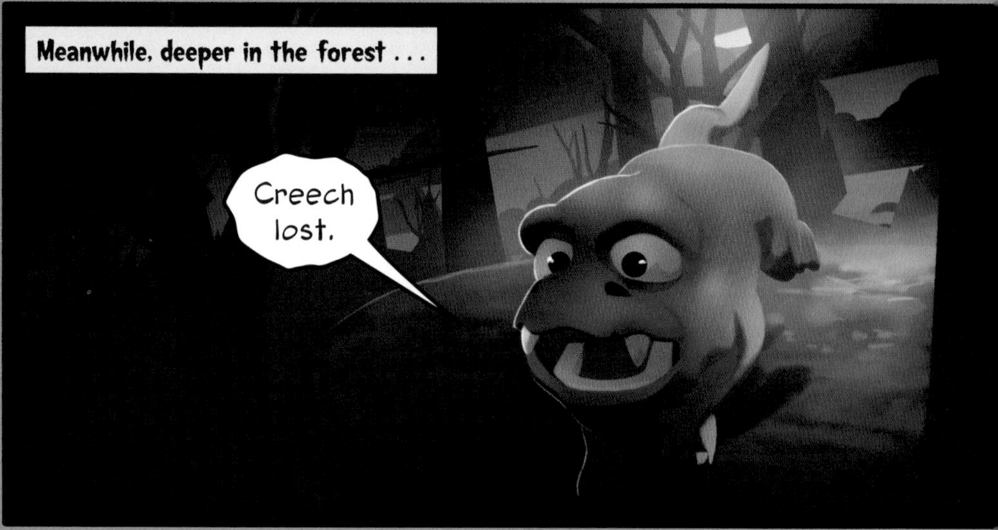
Meanwhile, deeper in the forest . . .
Creech lost.

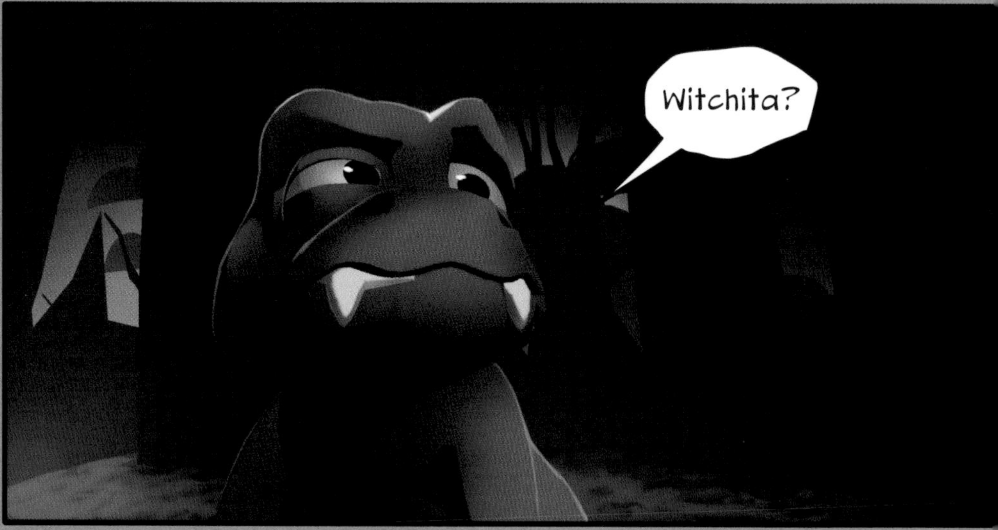
Witchita?

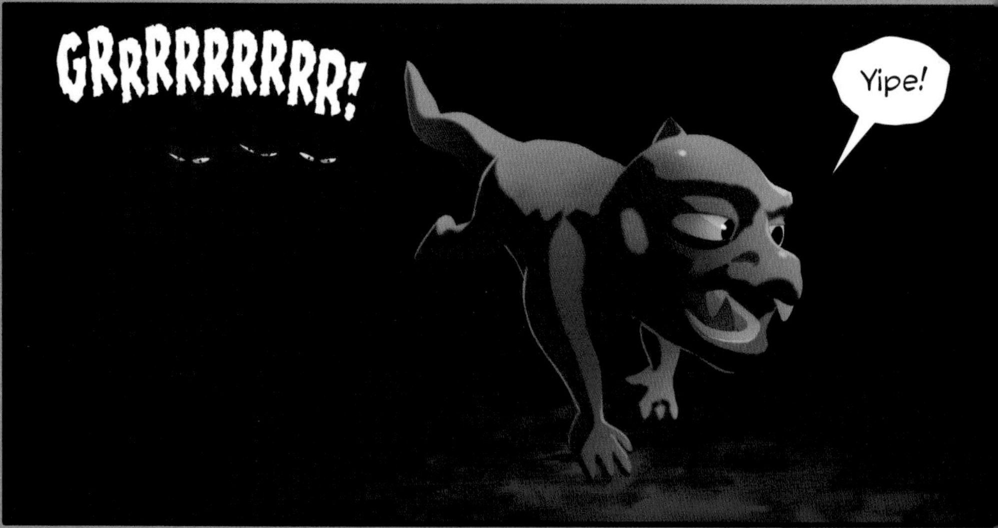
GRRRRRRRRR!
Yipe!

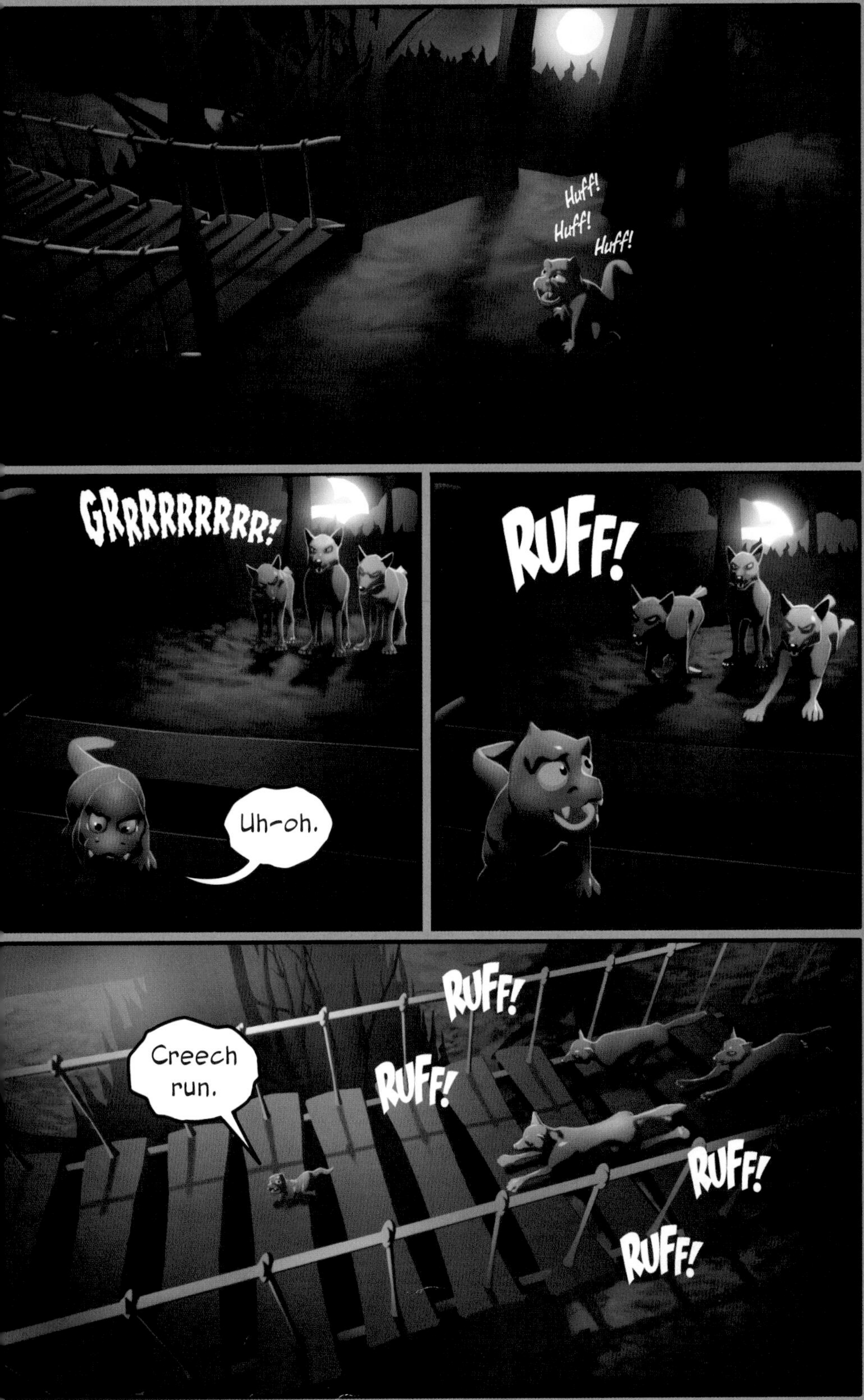
Huff!
Huff!
Huff!
GRRRRRRRRR!
Uh-oh.
RUFF!
Creech run.
RUFF!
RUFF!
RUFF!
RUFF!

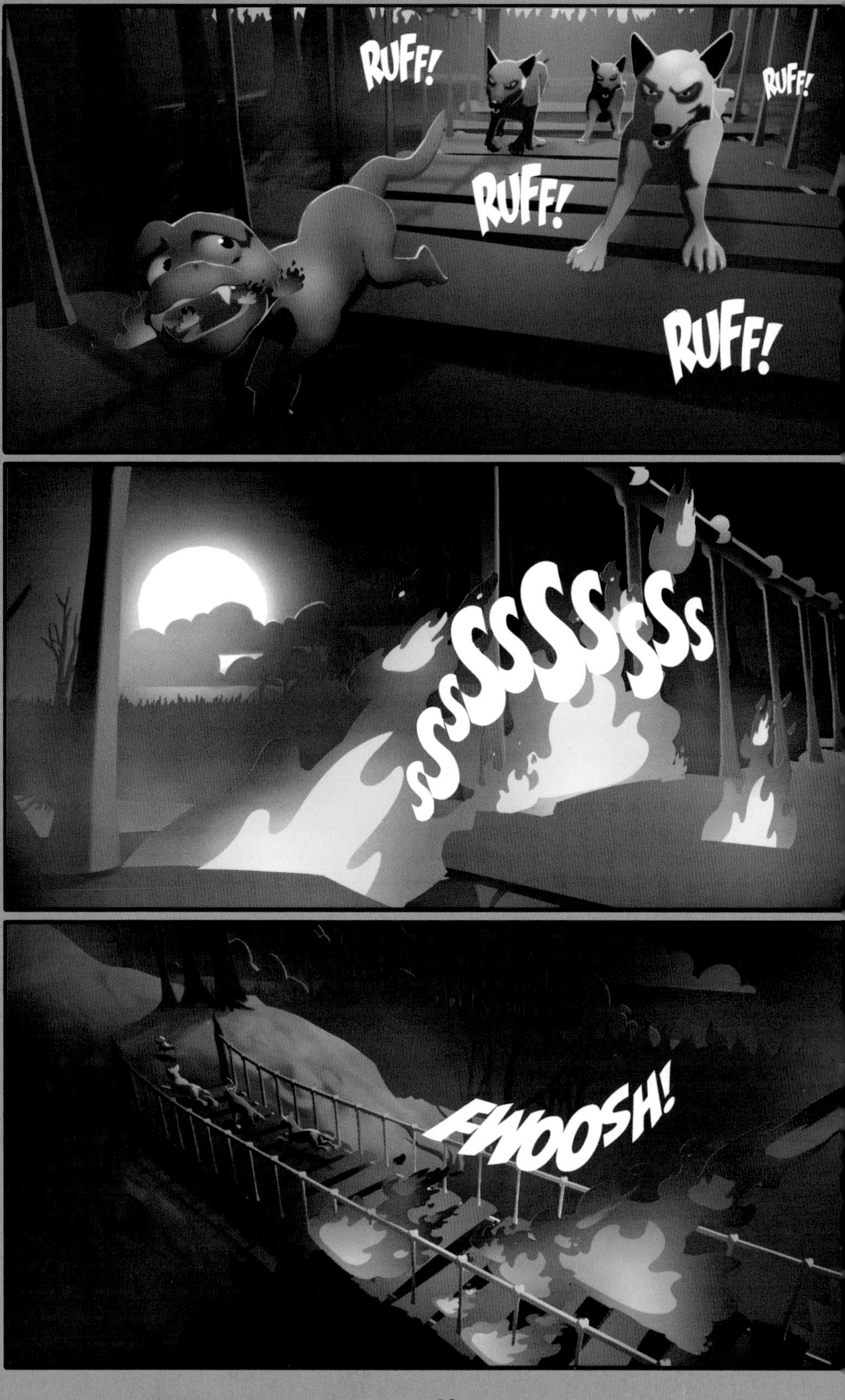
RUFF!
RUFF!
RUFF!
RUFF!
sSSSSSSSSs
FWOOSH!

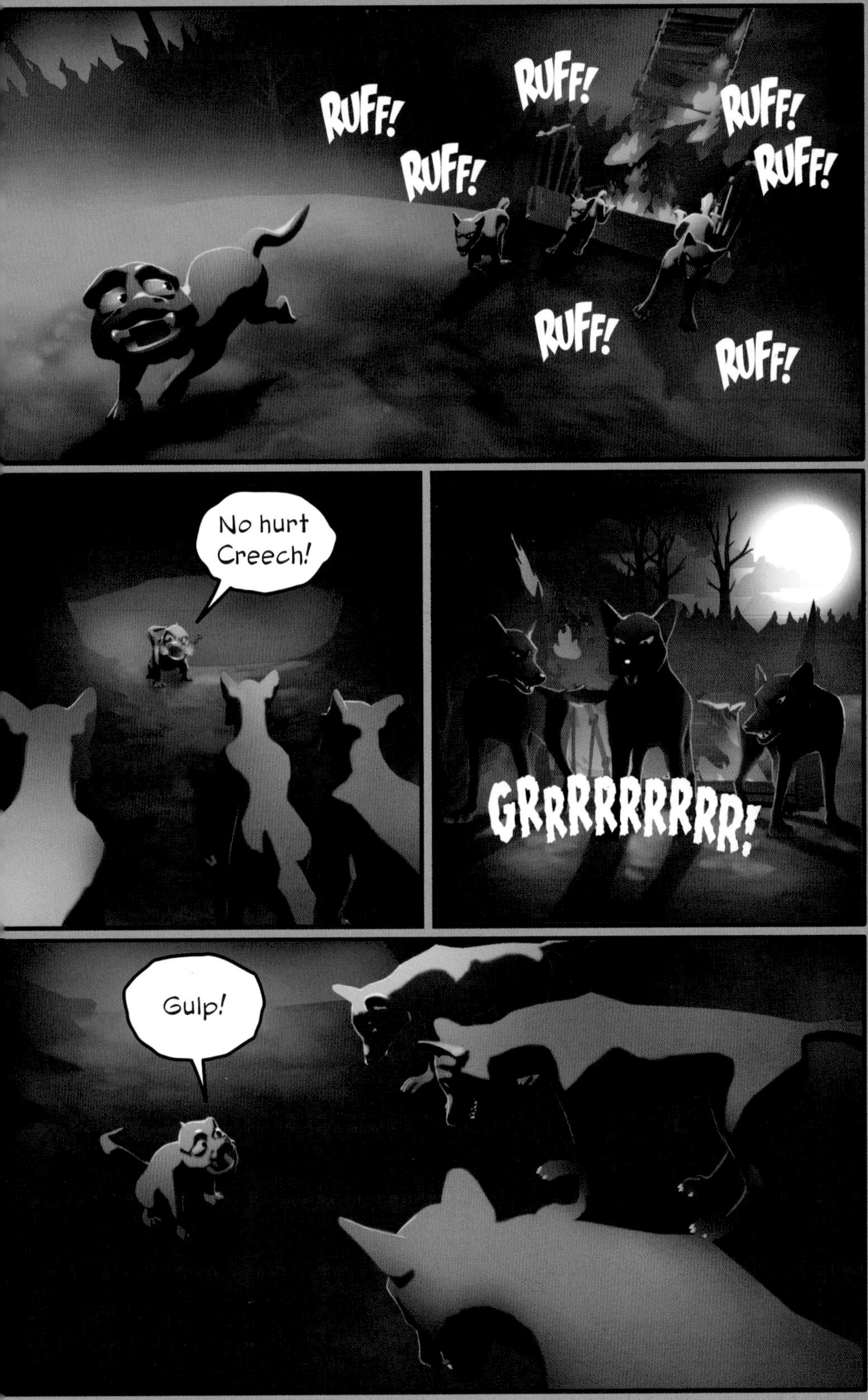
RUFF!
RUFF!
RUFF!
RUFF!
RUFF!
RUFF!
RUFF!
No hurt Creech!
GRRRRRRRRRR!
Gulp!

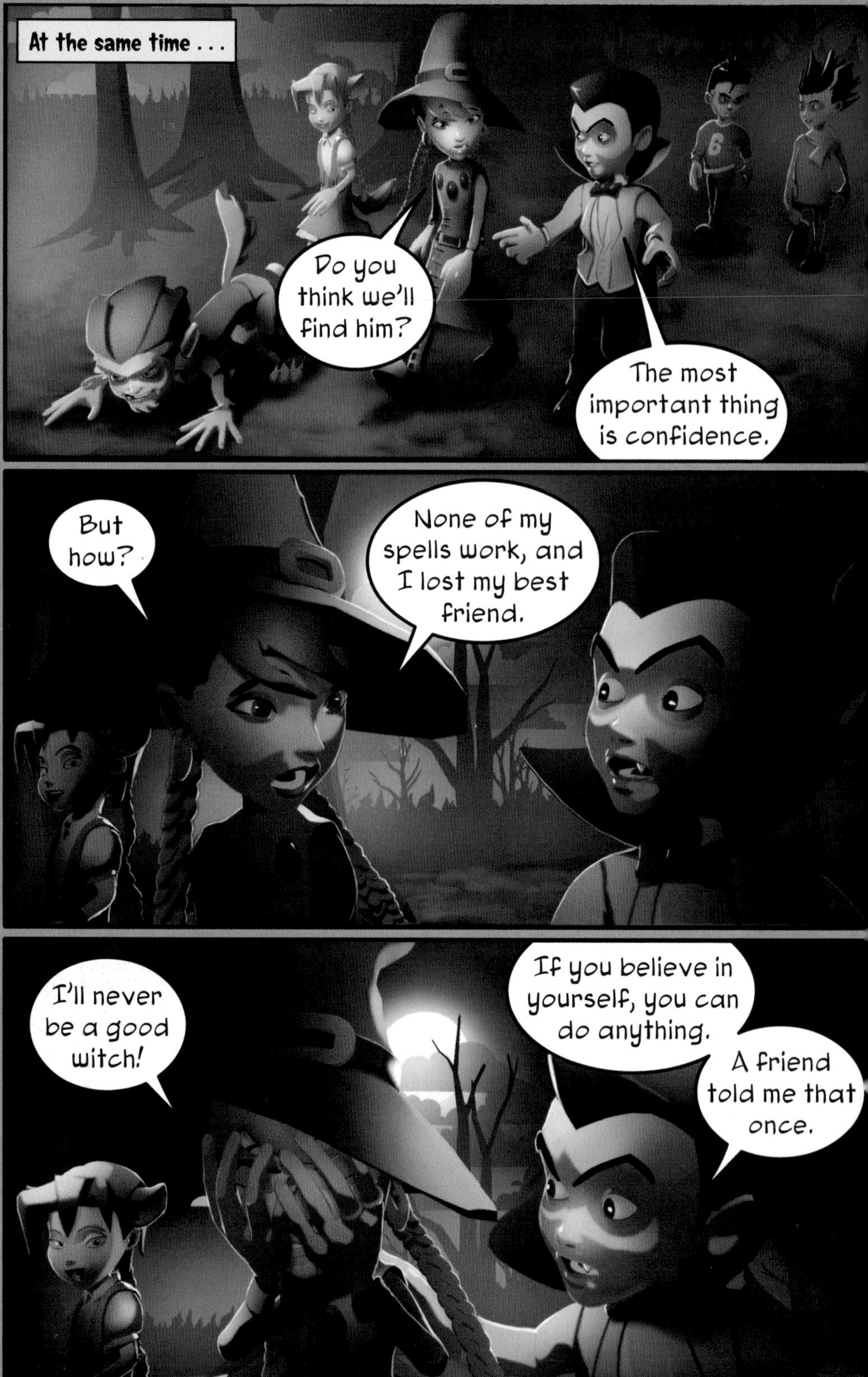
At the same time . . .
Do you think we'll find him?
The most important thing is confidence.
But how?
None of my spells work, and I lost my best friend.
I'll never be a good witch!
If you believe in yourself, you can do anything.
A friend told me that once.

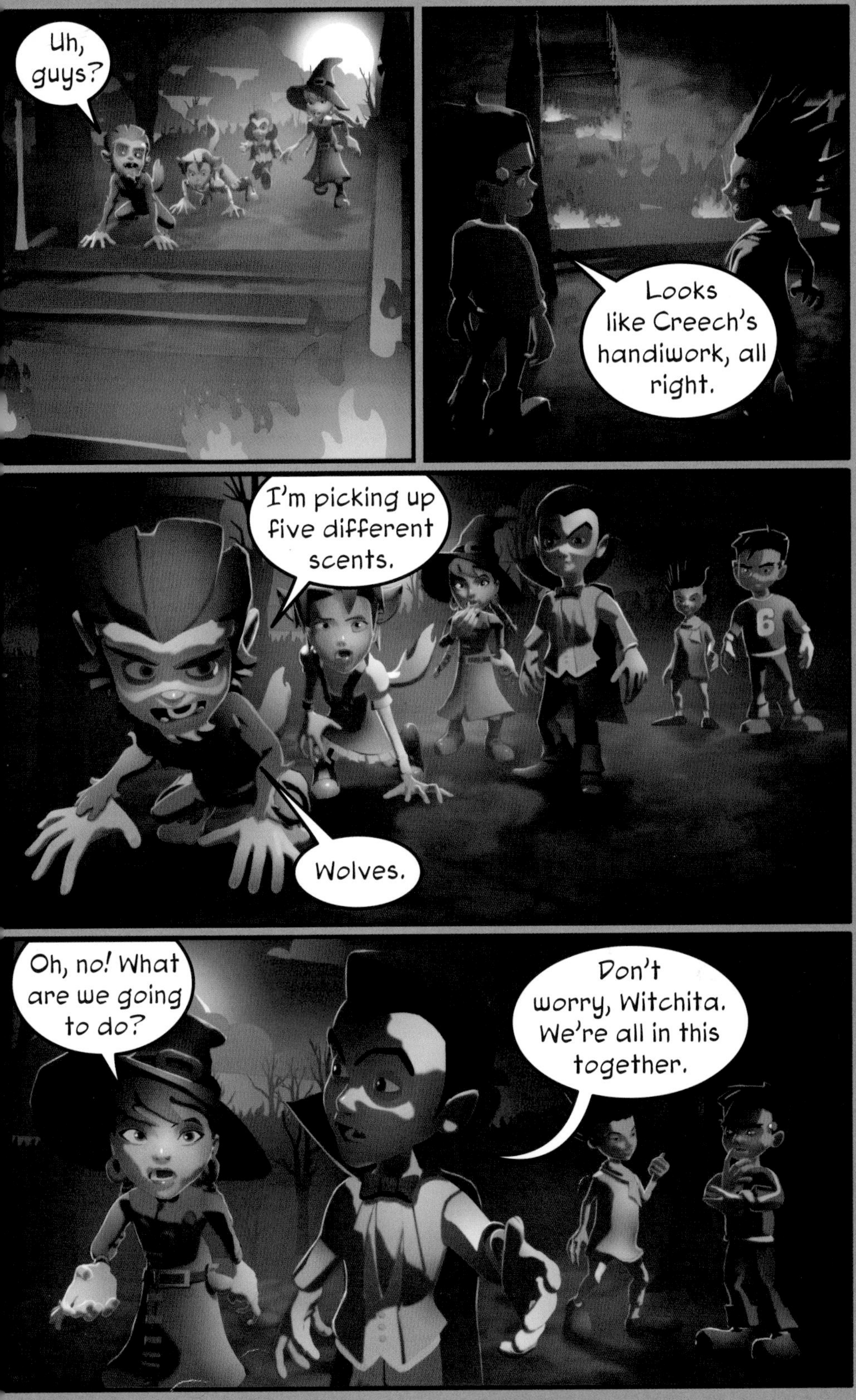
Uh, guys?
Looks like Creech's handiwork, all right.
I'm picking up five different scents.
Wolves.
Oh, no! What are we going to do?
Don't worry, Witchita. We're all in this together.

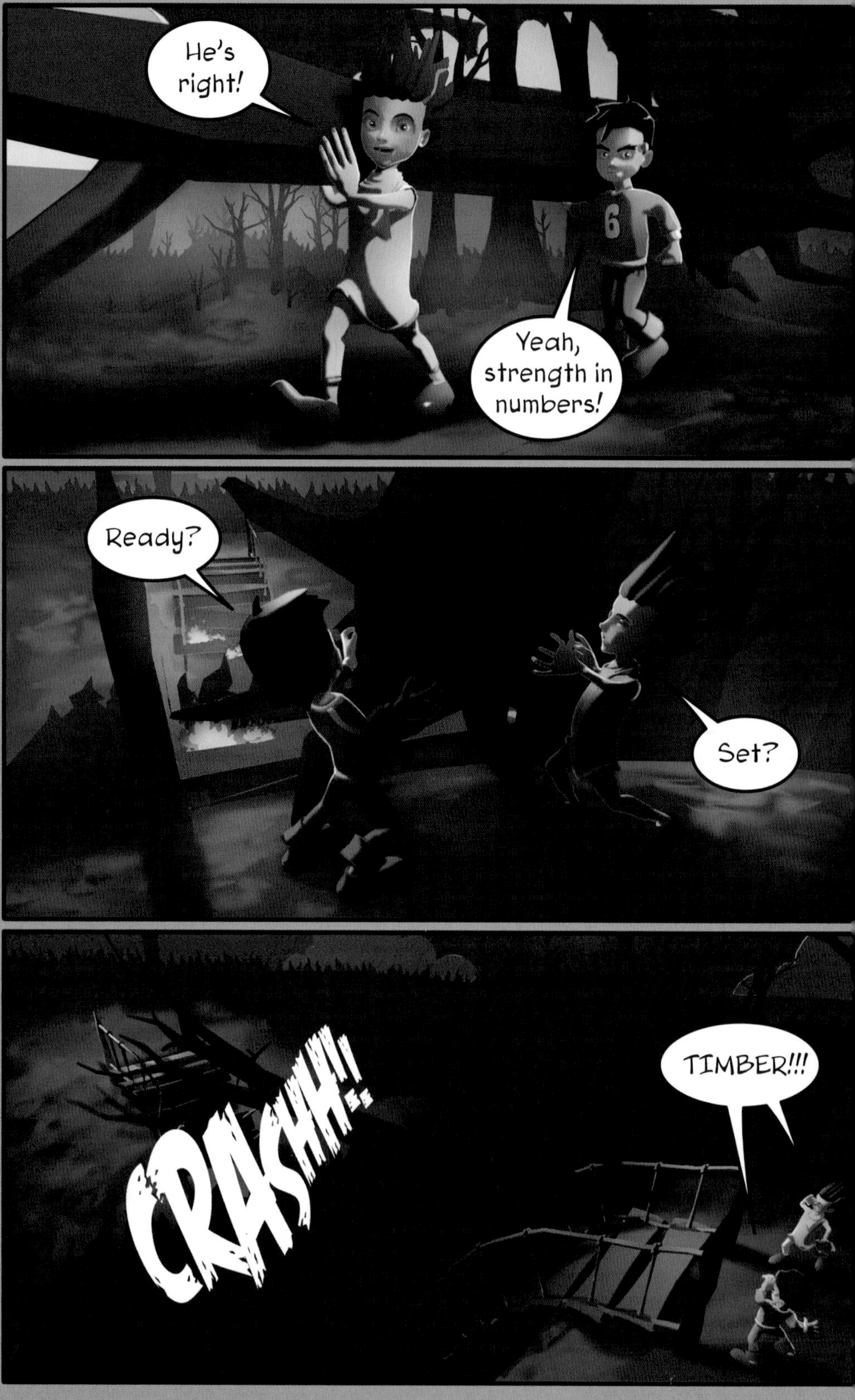
He's right!
Yeah, strength in numbers!
Ready?
Set?
CRASHH!!
TIMBER!!!

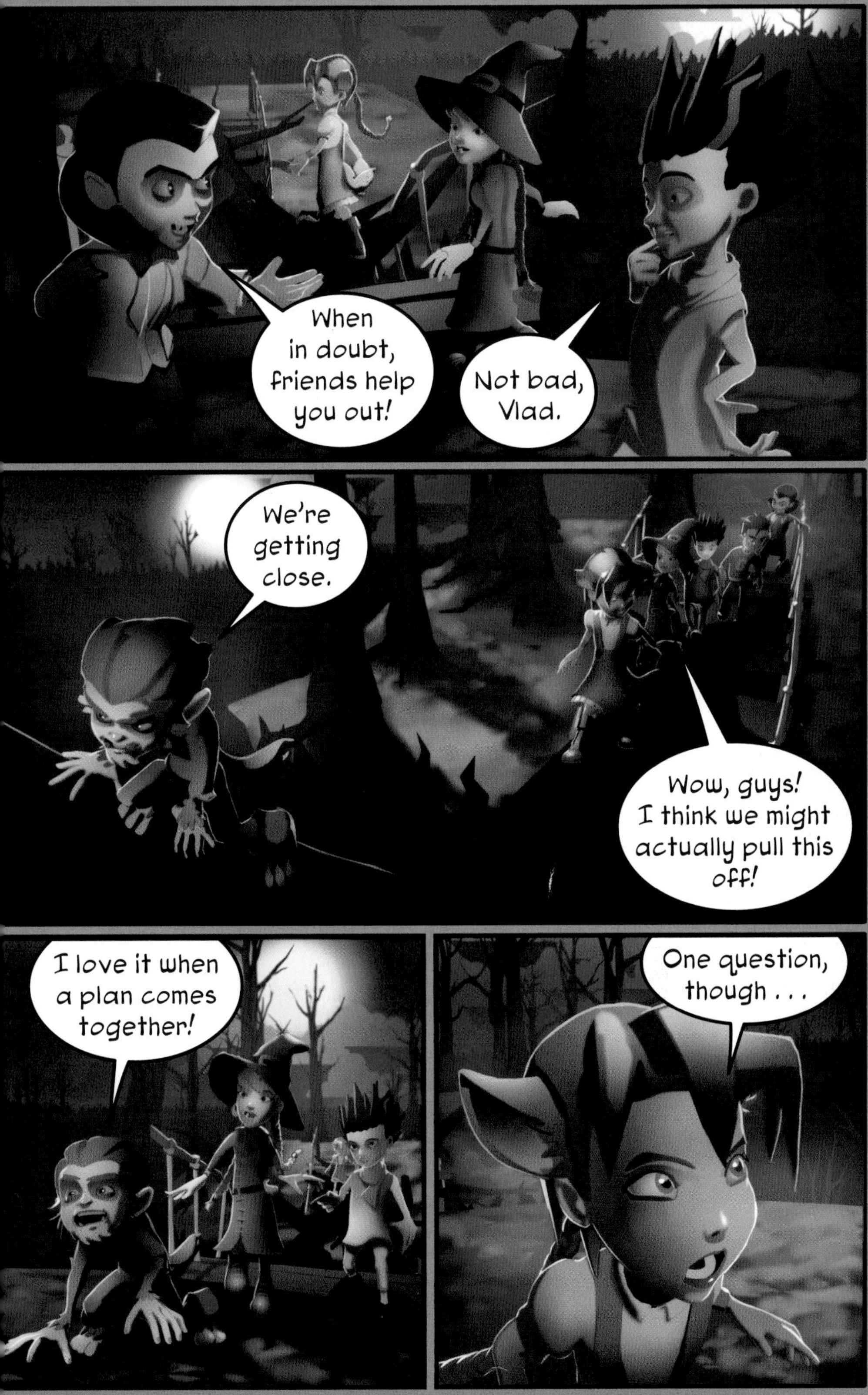

When in doubt, friends help you out!
Not bad, Vlad.
We're getting close.
Wow, guys! I think we might actually pull this off!
I love it when a plan comes together!
One question, though . . .

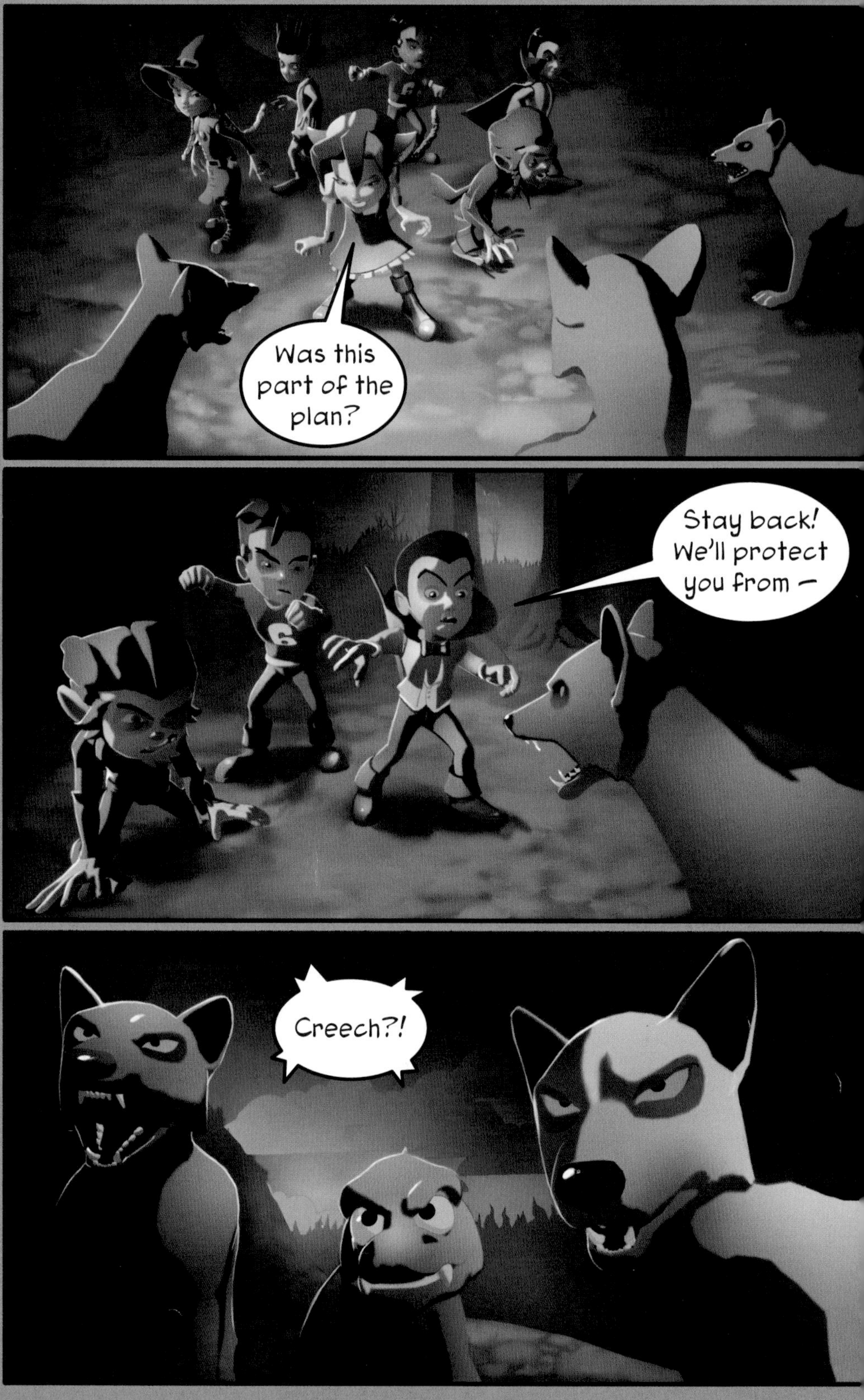
Was this part of the plan?
Stay back! We'll protect you from —
Creech?!

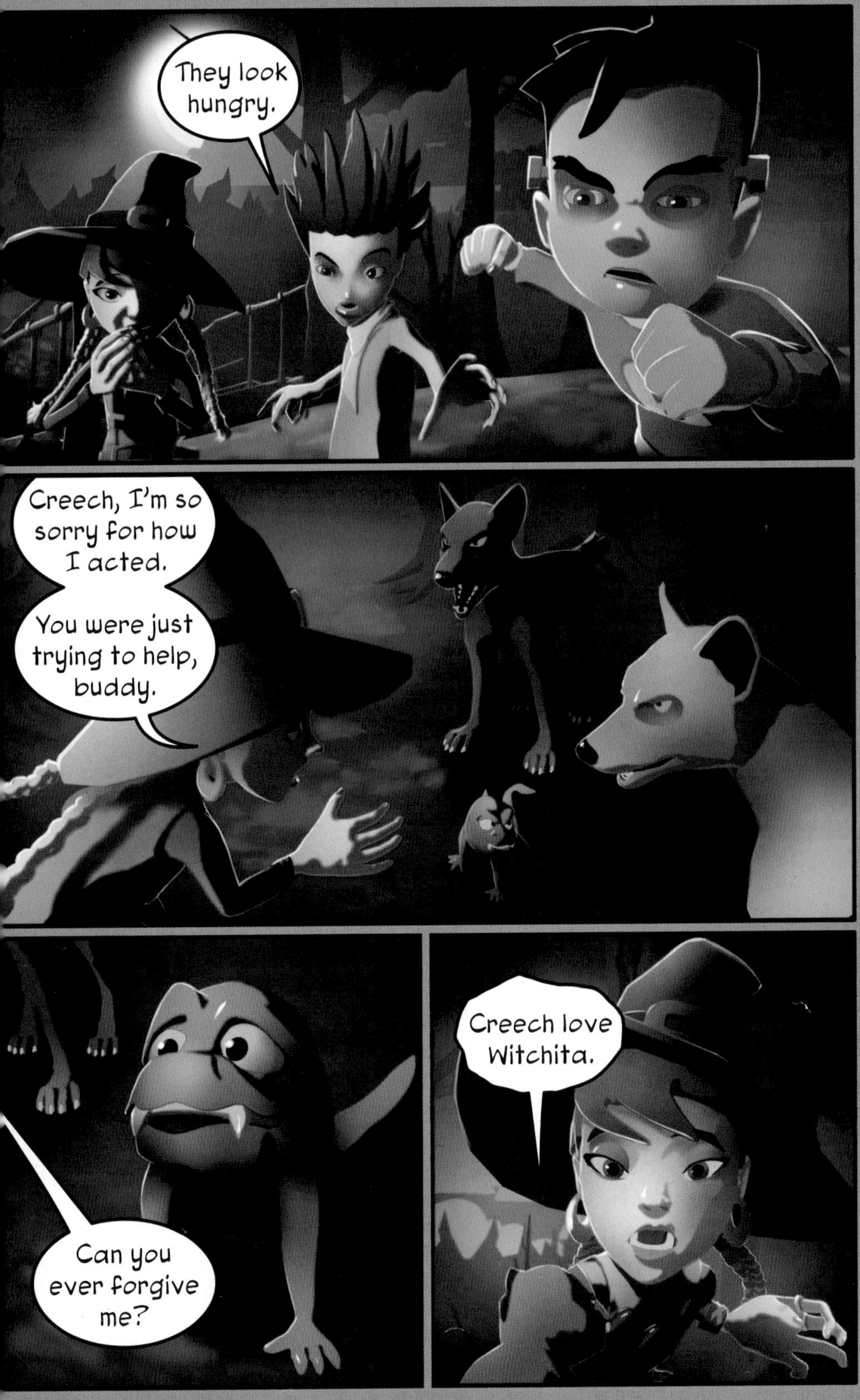
They look hungry.
Creech, I'm so sorry for how I acted.
You were just trying to help, buddy.
Can you ever forgive me?
Creech love Witchita.

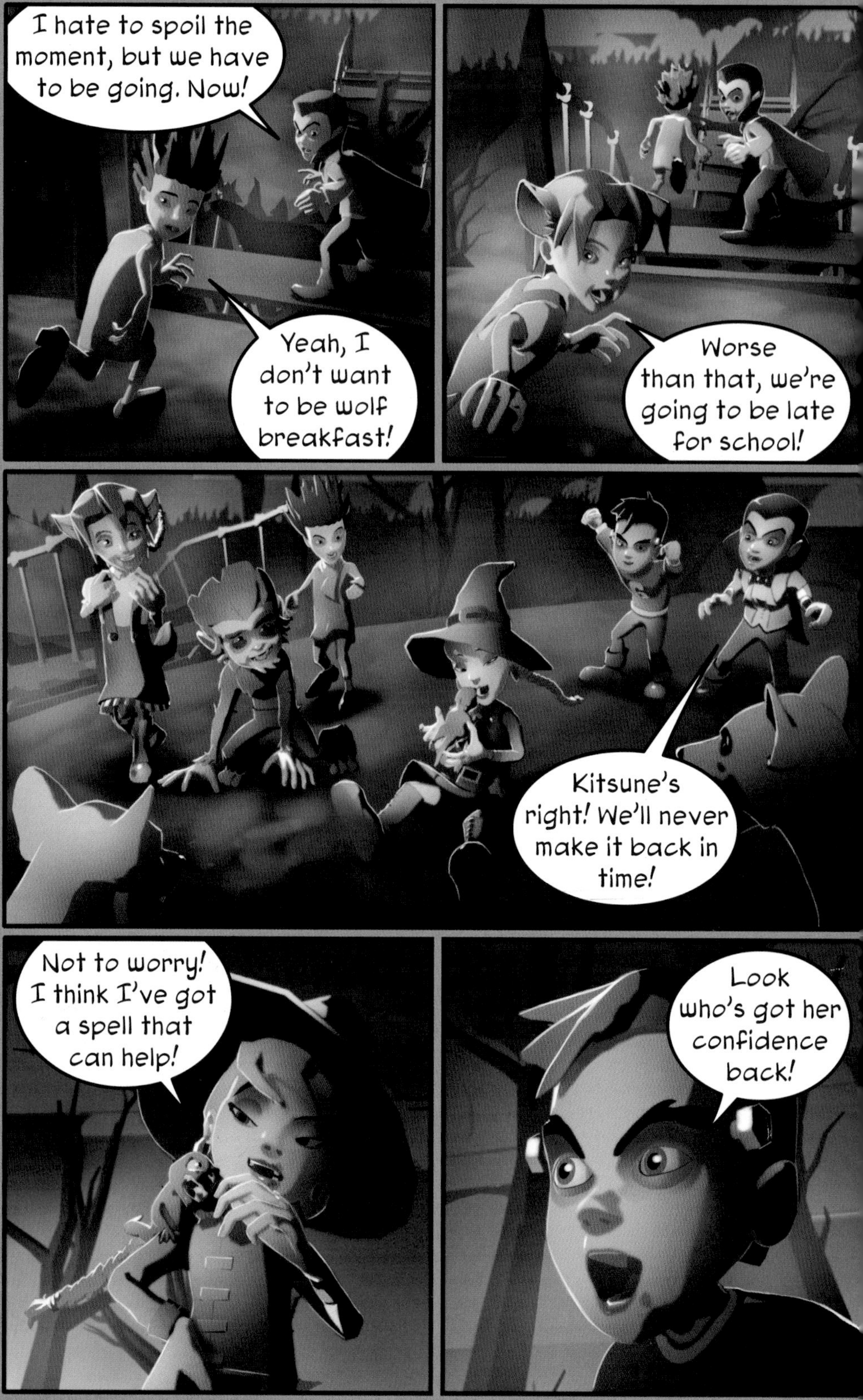
I hate to spoil the moment, but we have to be going. Now!
Yeah, I don't want to be wolf breakfast!
Worse than that, we're going to be late for school!
Kitsune's right! We'll never make it back in time!
Not to worry! I think I've got a spell that can help!
Look who's got her confidence back!

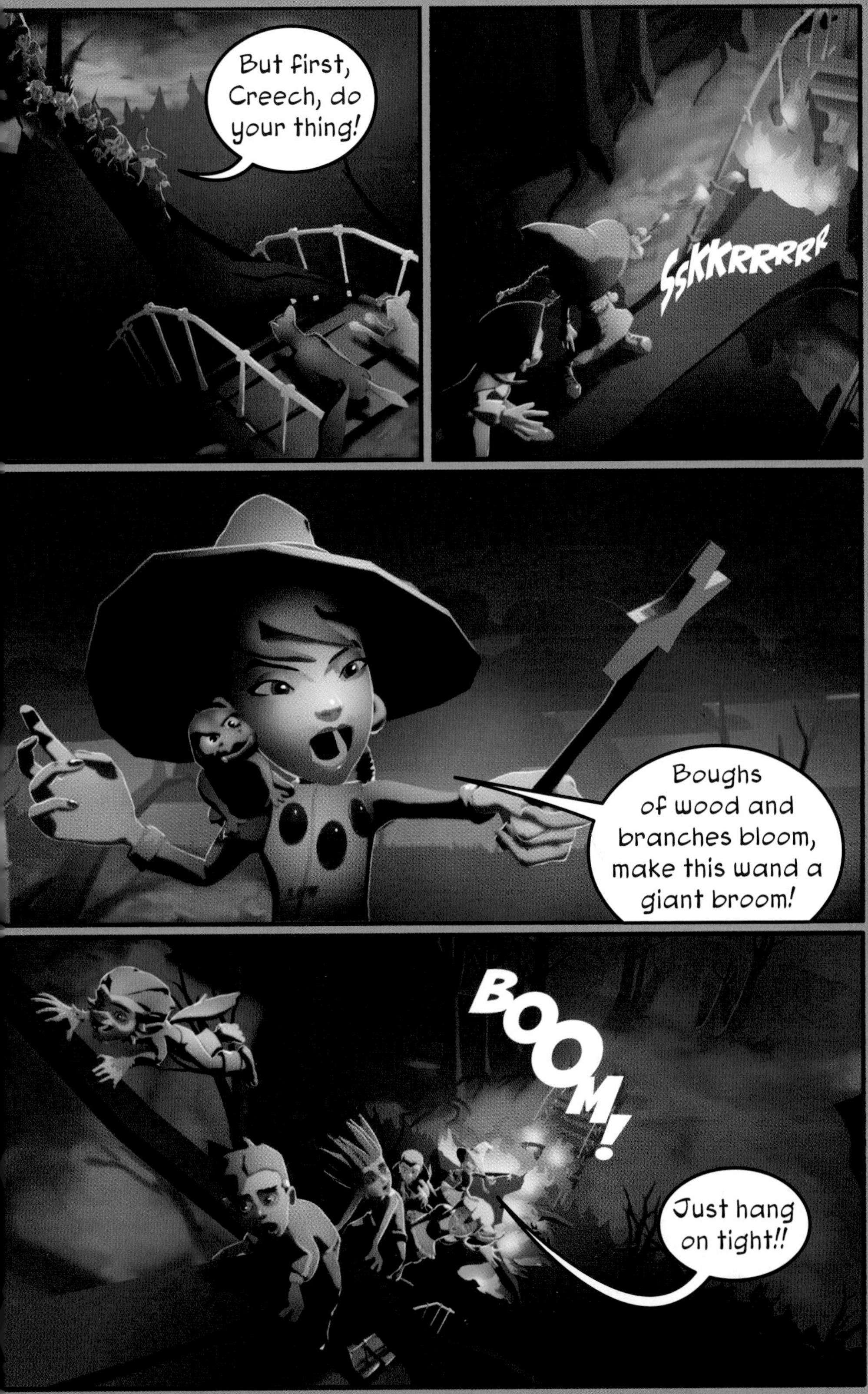
But first, Creech, do your thing!
SSKKRRRRR
Boughs of wood and branches bloom, make this wand a giant broom!
BOOM!
Just hang on tight!!

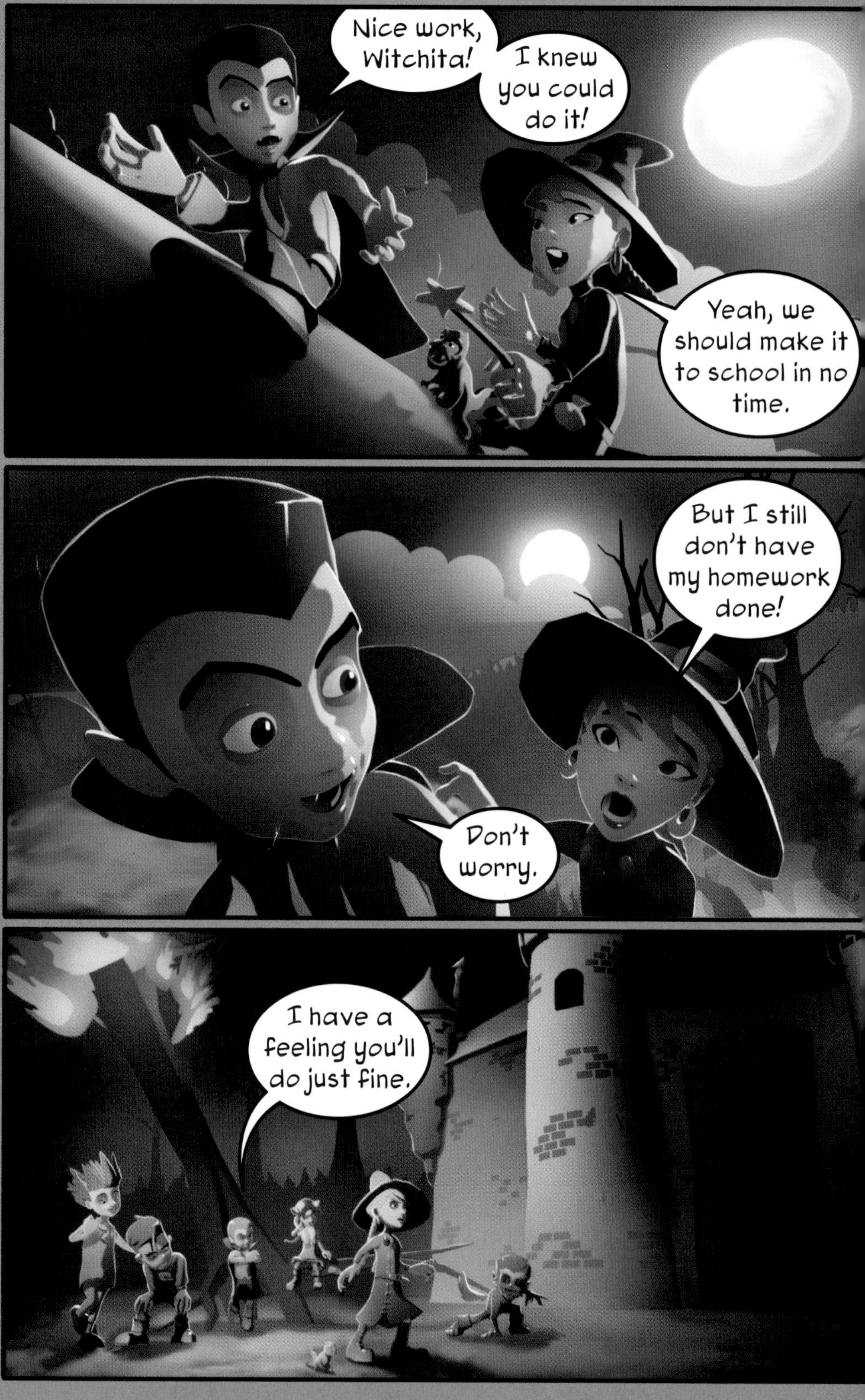
Nice work, Witchita!
I knew you could do it!
Yeah, we should make it to school in no time.
But I still don't have my homework done!
Don't worry.
I have a feeling you'll do just fine.

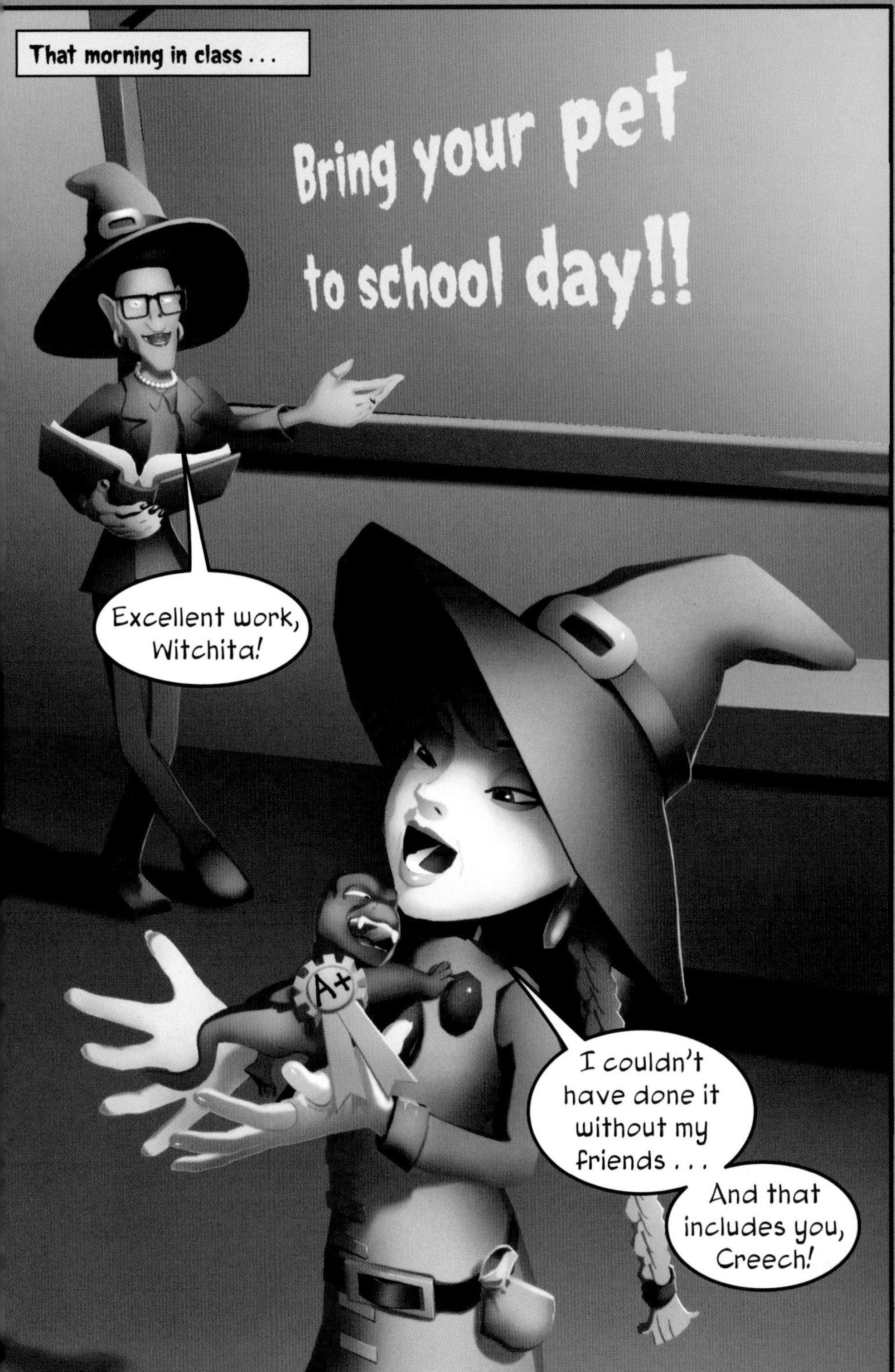
That morning in class . . .
Bring your pet to school day!!
Excellent work, Witchita!
A+
I couldn't have done it without my friends . . .
And that includes you, Creech!

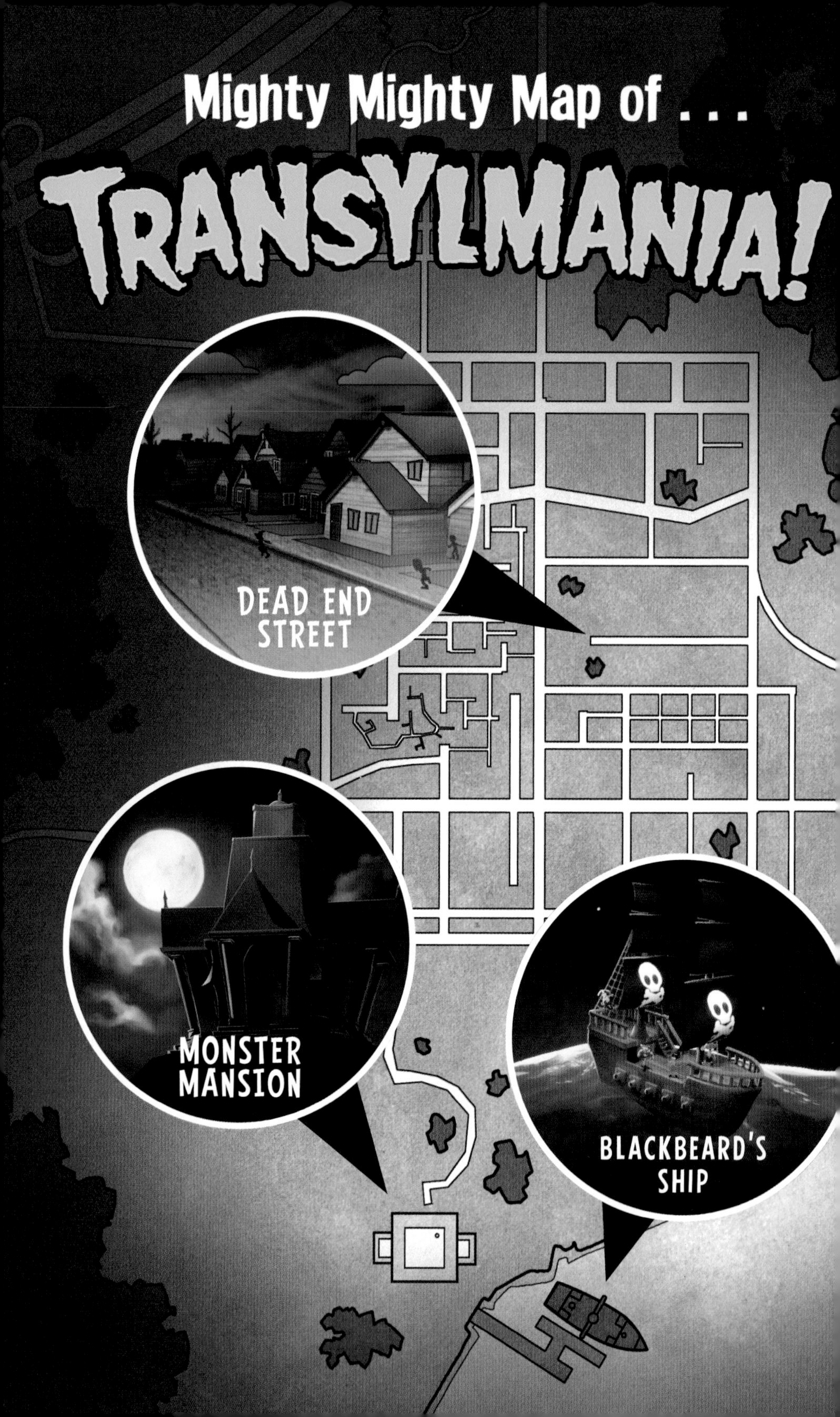
Mighty Mighty Map of . . .
TRANSYLMANIA!
DEAD END STREET
MONSTER MANSION
BLACKBEARD'S SHIP

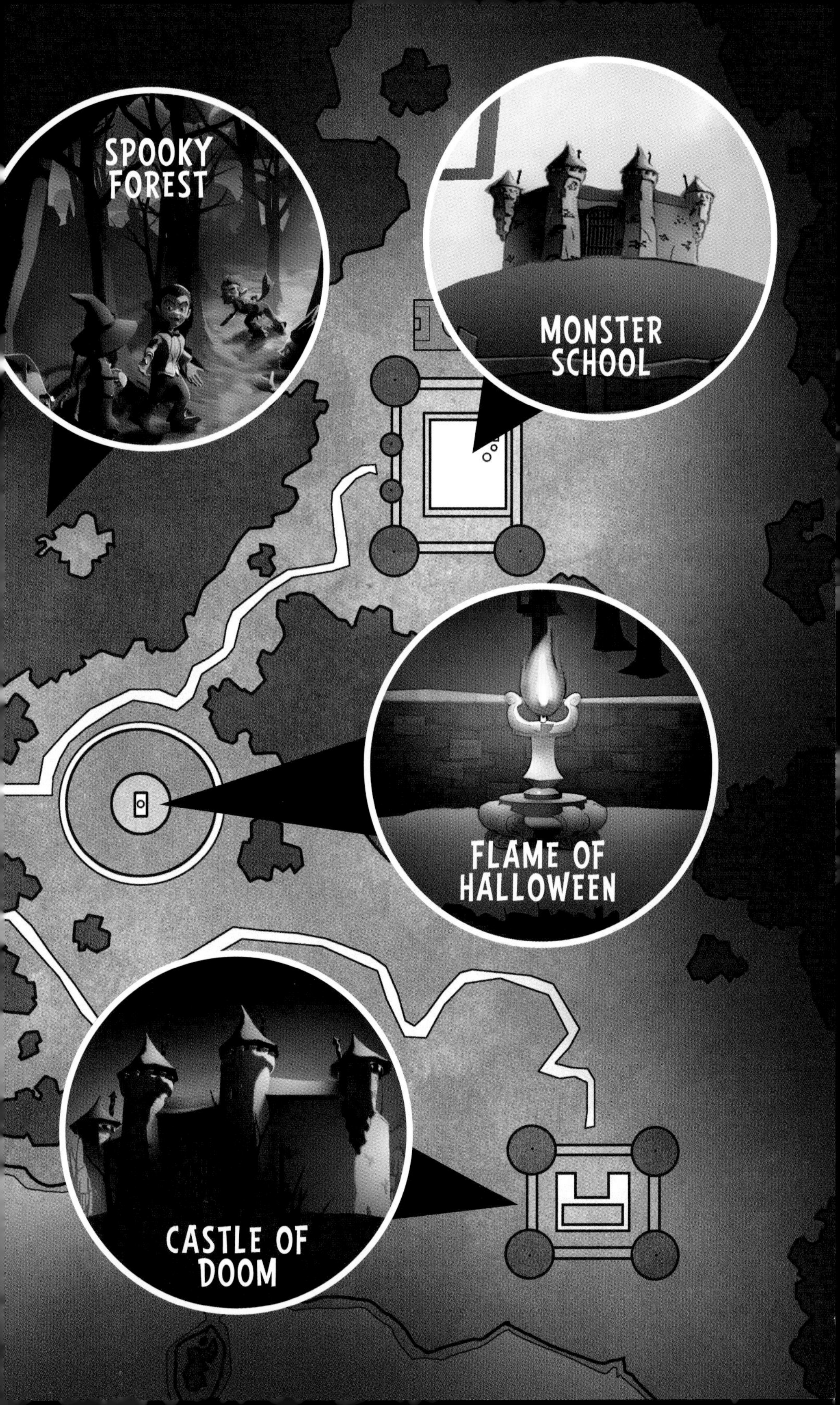
SPOOKY FOREST
MONSTER SCHOOL
FLAME OF HALLOWEEN
CASTLE OF DOOM

Mighty Mighty MONSTERS

...BEFORE THEY WERE STARS!

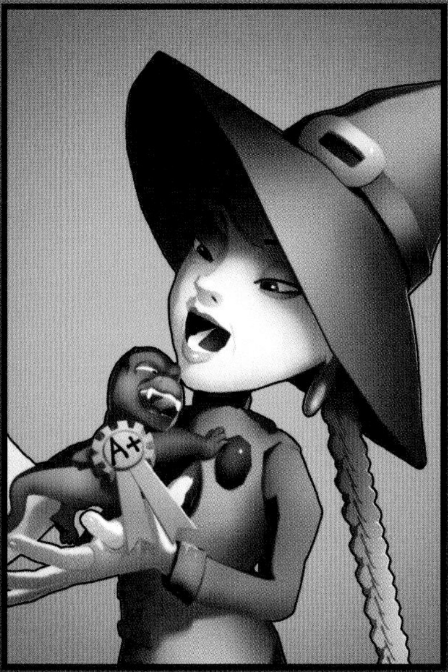
A+

WITCHITA AND CREECH

Nicknames: Witchy and Fire Breath

Hometown: Transylmania

Favorite Color: Black

Favorite Animal: Black Cats

Mighty Mighty Powers: Witchita has magical superpowers; Creech has the ability to breathe fire; together, they are unstoppable.

BIOGRAPHY

As a young magic maker, Witchita struggled to control her powers. At age two, she turned her babysitter into a cockroach. Unfortunately, these early failures left Witchita with little confidence. But, as a member of the Mighty Mighty Monsters, she quickly got it back. Along with her super pet Creech, Witchita is one of the most powerful members of the ghoulish gang. As an adult, Witchita headed to Hollywood, where she instructed some of the greatest witches of all time.

WHERE ARE THEY NOW?

Author L. Frank Baum created the Wicked Witch of the West for his children's book *The Wonderful Wizard of Oz*. In 1931, the book was adapted into a movie, making the character one of the scariest witches of all time.

Of course, not all witches are evil. In his children's book, Baum also created two good witches: The Good Witch of the South and the Good Witch of the North. However, only the latter appears in the film adaptation.

Today, witches are still popular in books and films. In J. K. Rowling's bestselling *Harry Potter* series, students study to become wizards and witches.

About Sean O'Reilly
and Arcana Studio

As a lifelong comics fan, Sean O'Reilly dreamed of becoming a comic book creator. In 2004, he realized that dream by creating Arcana Studio. In one short year, O'Reilly took his studio from a one-person operation in his basement to an award-winning comic book publisher with more than 150 graphic novels produced for Harper Collins, Simon & Schuster, Random House, Scholastic, and others.

Within a year, the company won many awards including the Shuster Award for Outstanding Publisher and the Moonbeam Award for top children's graphic novel. O'Reilly also won the Top 40 Under 40 award from the city of Vancouver and authored *The Clockwork Girl* for Top Graphic Novel at Book Expo America in 2009.

Currently, O'Reilly is one of the most prolific independent comic book writers in Canada. While showing no signs of slowing down in comics, he now writes screenplays and adapts his creations for the big screen.

GLOSSARY

accomplish (uh-KOM-plish)—to do something successfully

announcements (uh-NOUNSS-ments)—things said officially or publicly, as over a radio or loudspeaker

confidence (KON-fuh-denss)—a strong belief in your own abilities

DJ (DEE JAY)—short for "disc jockey," or an announcer on a radio show

excuse (ek-SKYOOS)—a reason given to explain why you have done something wrong

forecast (FOR-kast)—a prediction of what will happen in the future

laundry (LAWN-dree)—clothes, towels, sheets, and other items that are about to be washed

scent (SENT)—the odor trail left by an animal

talent (TAL-uhnt)—a natural ability or skill

tardy (TAR-dee)—not on time, such as being late for a class

tone deaf (TOHN DEF)—unable to hear the difference in musical pitch

DISCUSSION QUESTIONS

1. All of the Mighty Mighty Monsters helped Witchita find her pet. Which team member helped the most? Explain your answer.

2. Each page of this graphic novel has several illustrations. These illustrations are called panels. Which panel in this book is your favorite? Why?

3. All of the Mighty Mighty Monsters are different. Which character do you like the best? Why?

WRITING PROMPTS

1. Have you ever had a pet? If so, write a story about your pet. If not, write about a pet that you would like to have.

2. In this story, the Mighty Mighty Monsters helped out a friend. Describe a time that you helped a friend or family member.

3. Write your own Mighty Mighty Monsters adventure. What will the ghoulish gang do next? What villains will they face? You decide.

ighty Mighty ONSTERS

ADVENTURES

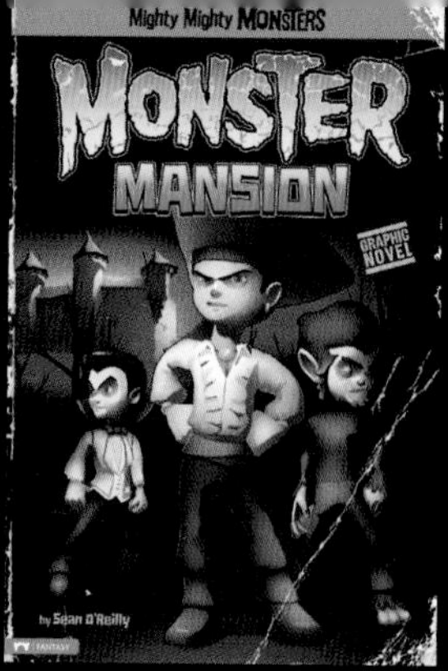
Mighty Mighty MONSTERS
MONSTER MANSION
GRAPHIC NOVEL
by Sean O'Reilly
FANTASY

Monster Mansion

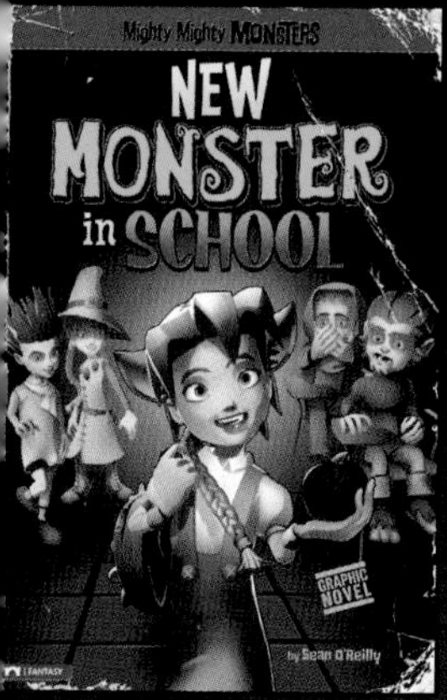
Mighty Mighty MONSTERS
NEW MONSTER in SCHOOL
GRAPHIC NOVEL
by Sean O'Reilly
FANTASY

New Monster in School

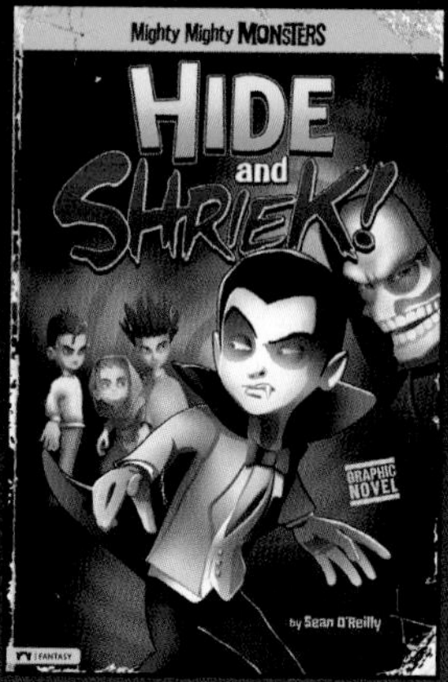
Mighty Mighty MONSTERS
HIDE and SHRIEK!
GRAPHIC NOVEL
by Sean O'Reilly
FANTASY

Hide and Shriek

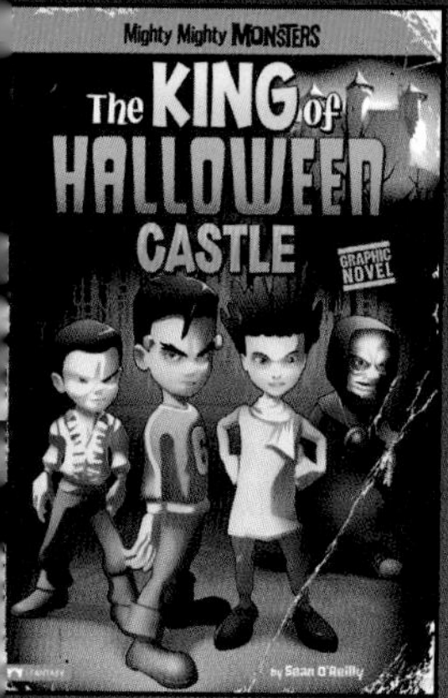
Mighty Mighty MONSTERS
The KING of HALLOWEEN CASTLE
GRAPHIC NOVEL
by Sean O'Reilly

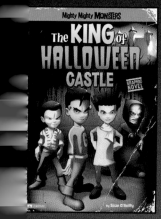

The King of Halloween Castle

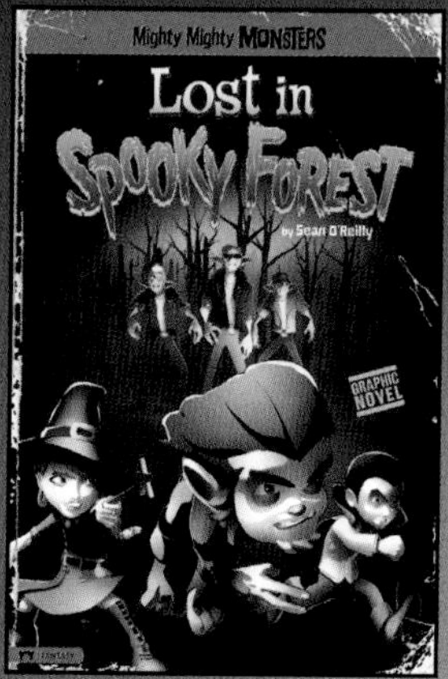
Mighty Mighty MONSTERS
Lost in Spooky Forest
by Sean O'Reilly
GRAPHIC NOVEL

Lost in Spooky Forest

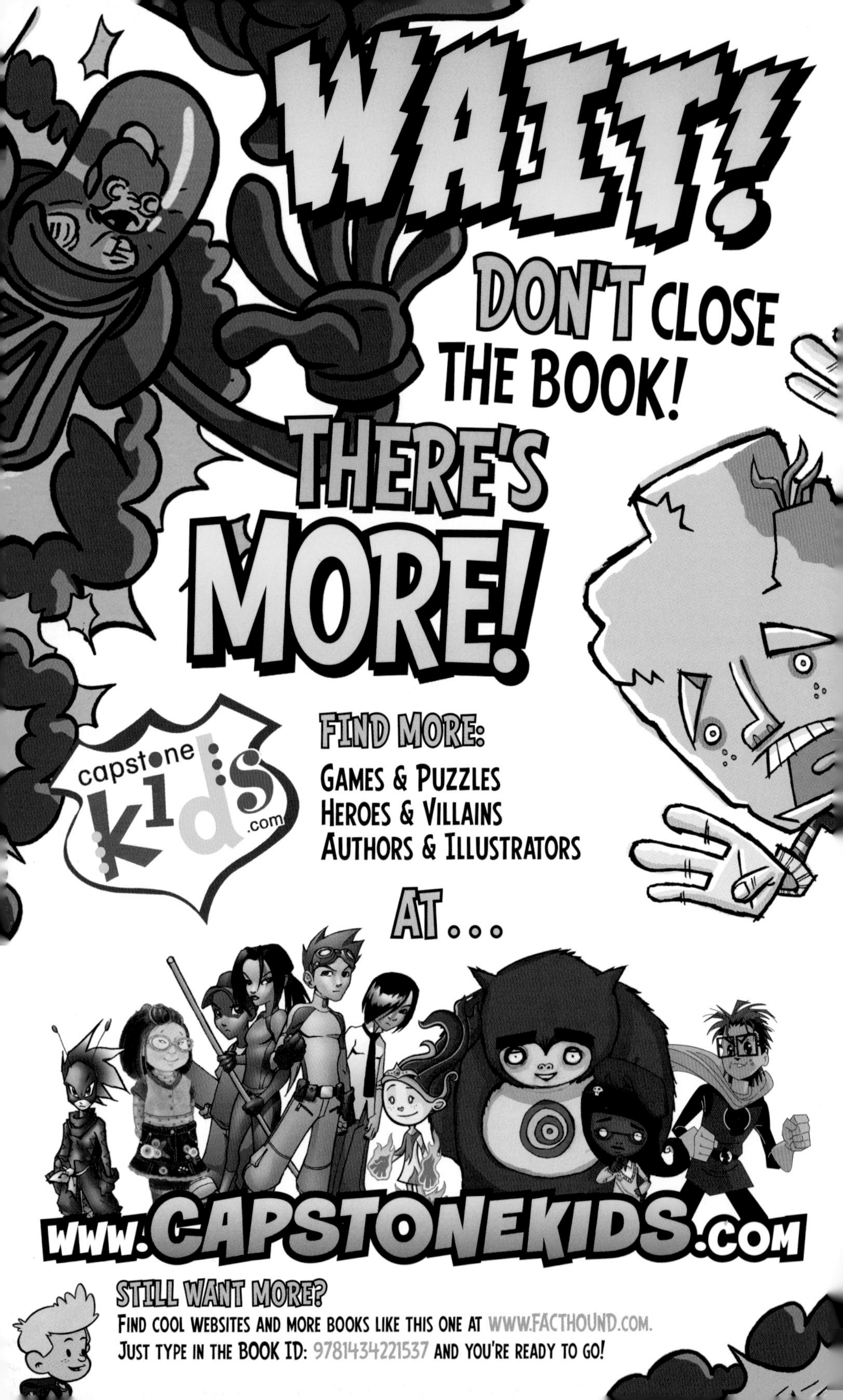
WAIT!
DON'T CLOSE THE BOOK!
THERE'S MORE!
capstone kids .com
FIND MORE:
GAMES & PUZZLES
HEROES & VILLAINS
AUTHORS & ILLUSTRATORS
AT...
WWW.CAPSTONEKIDS.COM
STILL WANT MORE?
FIND COOL WEBSITES AND MORE BOOKS LIKE THIS ONE AT WWW.FACTHOUND.COM.
JUST TYPE IN THE BOOK ID: 9781434221537 AND YOU'RE READY TO GO!